Renew

A Second Chance WorkPlace Contemporary Romance

Heart of Stone Jessica and Joseph
Book 4

Chiquita Dennie

304 Publishing Company

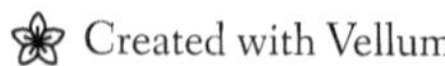 Created with Vellum

Latest Releases

The Early Years-A Prequel Short Story
 Struck in Love 1, 2, 3,4,5
 Heart of Stone, Book 1 (Emery & Jackson)
 Heart Of Stone Book 1.5 Emery &Jackson A Valentine's Day Short
 Janice and Carlo: Captivated By His Love
 Heart of Stone, Book 2 (Jordan and Damon)
 Temptation
 Heart of Stone, Book 3 (Angela and Brent)
 Bottoms Up Heart of Stone, Book 3.5(Jessica and Joseph Short
 Cocky Catcher
 Bossy Billionaire
 Love Shorts:A Collection of Short Stories
 Stolen Fuertes Mafia Cartel Book 1
 Saved Fuertes Mafia Cartel Book 2
 Exposed (Salvation Society Novel)
 Betrayal Fuertes Mafia Cartel Book 3
 Refuel(A Driven World Novel)
 Pressure(A Driven World Novel)

Until Serena(HEA World Novel)
Exposed (Salvation Society Novel)
Heart of Stone, Book 4 (Jessica and Joseph)
She's All I Need
Something Gaine(Romantic Comedy)
Upcoming Releases (2023/2024):
Something Earned (Romantic Comedy)
The Carrington Cartel
Nicco-TN Seal Security Book 3
Something Borrowed(Romantic Comedy
Knox-TN Seal Security Book 4

For my Family

I want to dedicate this book to my family, and friends. Always with me no matter where I go and everything you've taught me has made me a better person.

Disclaimer

This work of fiction contains strong language and explicit sexual content and is only intended for mature readers. This story may contain unconventional situations, language, and sexual encounters that may offend some readers. If you're looking for sweet, fluffy romance, I would recommend another book. This book is for mature readers (18+).

Introduction

Grab some wine and get ready for more spicy, sinful, sexy romance.

Are you signed up for my newsletter?

Join today and find out all the latest in new releases, contests, giveaways, sneak peeks and more.
www.chiquitadennie.com

Synopsis

I thought that I loved the single life… until I met him.

Joseph:

Leave it to me to choose to fall in love with a girl that has commitment issues.

Jessica is perfect for me though.

I'm ready to settle down and claim my happily ever after with her.

Now I just need to convince her that being with me and settling down is the right choice.

Jessica:

I never understood romance movies.

They always made being single look so bad, but I don't see it that way.

Being wined and dined, having no strings attached relationships has always been perfect for me.

Until I meet Joseph.

One night with him and I want more.

That's never happened before and now I'm left wondering if maybe I had it wrong all these years.

Will Jessica be able to let down her walls and trust that her and Joseph are meant to be?

Chapter 1

Jessica

Seven **Months Later**

We decorated the house with red-and-gold balloons, her favorite colors, and had Emery take her out to church for bingo, so we could finish last-minute details. We found some of her favorite records and had them playing, along with the latest music.

The lights were turned off, and I scooted behind the couch and bent down to hide. I said to Angela earlier that this would not be a good idea, but she insisted on making a big deal about surprising Granny for her birthday. A few months ago, Emery had come to us about throwing a surprise party, and since I was still in the middle of dealing with my stupid ex, and my emotions for Joseph, I'd said I could help. I'd needed something to distract me from making a fool of myself for Eric again.

"Shush... I hear the car pulling up," Angela said, and everyone quieted down.

The crowd was enormous and packed inside Pops' and Granny's house. They had stayed in the same house for over 40 years. Over time, Emery and Jackson had added a gazebo, a pool, and an extra bedroom for guests. I'd found myself hanging out more over here with them whenever I wasn't working, but I'd ended up getting a huge design job a month ago, and I wanted to focus on making sure that it was perfect.

"Granny, are you going to share your winnings?" I heard Emery ask.

"*Share?!* Child, be grateful that I feed you and your children," Granny said, and I giggled as the screen door opened. A key jingled, and the front door opened wide.

"Weren't you just complaining that I don't bring them over as much?" Emery complained.

The light flickered on. We jumped up and screamed. "Surprise!" All the guests cheered and clapped.

"Jesus! Y'all almost got your heads blown off," Granny argued with her hand inside her coat jacket, finger out, as if it were a gun.

"Old lady, take your hand out of your pocket. You aren't doing anything." Angela walked up to her with her arms out for a hug.

Granny pushed her away. "Shut up, Big Mama," Granny replied, and I burst into laughter.

Angela was pregnant again, and she was constantly cursing Brent out for it. This would be Baby #3. Brent was ecstatic about having a son. Ever since they got married, he had made it his mission to keep her knocked up. Their relationship had blossomed into something even more beautiful, like Emery and Jackson's.

"You hater," Angela responded and helped Granny out of her coat.

I strolled over to her with a cup in my hand and took a sip. "Happy birthday, Granny." I pressed a kiss on her cheek.

She grabbed my drink, smelled it, and had a sip, then stared back at me. "Ew, that's strong." Her brows dipped into a frown.

"And yet, you're still holding onto my cup."

"You mean *my* cup, since it's in my house." Granny pursed her lips together.

"Happy birthday, Granny. You don't look a day over 60," Brent said when he walked into her house.

The music turned back up, and I looked over her shoulder when he bent down to hug her. There, I saw the last person that I needed to see. My breathing picked up, and I snatched the cup out of her hand and gulped the last of the tequila and club soda.

Joseph looked just as sexy as he had at work two days ago. It was like we were complete strangers now—or maybe it was all in my head. His six-foot frame filled the room as he stepped in and went to give Granny a hug.

"Thank you, Brent. I told Angela that you're a good catch." Granny pinched his cheek.

"Stop flirting with my husband, Granny." Angela locked arms with Brent.

I looked around the room, trying to avoid eye contact.

"Happy birthday, Granny. Here's a little something for you." Joseph passed her a bouquet of flowers and a card.

"Thank you, baby. Aren't you nice to bring me a gift?" Granny said and pushed the flowers into my hands. She opened the birthday card with scratch-off tickets inside. She started smiling and trying to poke her butt out to dance. "See, I knew you were a great catch. I apologize about this one not seeing your worth," she said and pointed over at me.

My mouth dropped open in shock. Joseph shook his

head and grinned, and I closed my mouth, rubbing the top of my forehead. That woman was always embarrassing us.

"Granny, don't start," Angela said, interrupting the awkward moment.

JJ ran over and hugged Granny around the waist. "Happy birthday, Granny!" JJ called out. He was eight years old now and very much looked like his father, same as Brent and Damon. The women carried the kids, but they all came out looking like their husbands.

"Thank you, baby. Did you get me something?" she questioned.

JJ grinned and slid his hand into his pocket, then pulled out a small bag.

"Granny, don't you think you're too old to be asking for gifts from children?" Angela placed her hands on her hips and stared at Granny.

"Don't you think you're too old to be in my business?" Granny spat back.

We all burst into laughter as Angela rolled her eyes. Their back-and-forth would go on forever unless someone stopped them.

"I'm telling Pops," Angela remarked.

Granny opened the bag and pulled out a charm bracelet. "This is beautiful, baby." Granny bent down and kissed JJ on the forehead. He ran over to his mom.

I started to walk off to grab another drink at the bar. The crowd thickened as Granny hugged almost everyone in the room.

"That woman is so spoiled," Emery said, standing next to me.

"She went that way because of you and your husband." I twisted the lime in my drink and took another sip. I licked my lips and closed my eyes as the rum trailed down my throat.

"He still isn't talking to you?" Emery asked.

I opened one eye and peered at Emery. "Who?"

Jackson stepped into the living room from the kitchen and wrapped his arm around Emery. He rubbed the top of JJ's head.

"You know who," Emery said. "Stop playing dumb, Jessica." She grabbed a bottled water off the top of the bar.

"Are you about to have your talk about her screwed-up love life?" Jackson mentioned.

I scoffed at his comment. "I did *not* screw up my love life."

"Okay but listen to Emery's advice. She knows about screwing up relationships," Jackson said, and Emery punched him in the arm.

"That was one time. And look at us now—married with kids," Emery said.

I giggled at their back-and-forth. "How is work going?" I questioned, needing a distraction from conversations about romance.

"Busy and growing. We might open an Atlanta office," Jackson explained.

More kids ran over and sat in Granny's lap. Pops brought out a plate of food for her, and my stomach grumbled. I hadn't eaten anything since that morning. I'd started early on shopping for tonight, plus picking up food and chairs and making sure that I got her gifts. I'd decided to get her and Pops a gift certificate to their favorite restaurant, Charlie's.

"I think you should open one in London," Emery said.

Jackson playfully bent the side of her ear. "You'd be

ready to move, so you could shop every day," Jackson teased.

Emery stretched her arm around Jackson's neck and kissed him on the lips as Teena Marie and Rick James blasted loudly throughout the room.

"I'm going to grab something to eat." I walked around the two of them as they started making out like a couple of teenagers. I pushed through the crowd that was gathering in the living room, dancing and talking to Granny. I grabbed a plate off the table and lifted the top on the buffet tray. There was a host of items laid out: meatballs, chicken, spaghetti, potato salad, fries, and baked beans. Plus, alcohol for days. We only had the closest family and friends here.

"Are you hiding in here?"

I looked over my shoulder. Angela stepped in, rubbing her growing belly. "I was hungry."

"Mmm-hmm." Angela picked a hot wing off my plate and took a bite.

"Get your own plate."

She flipped me off and lifted a plate from the stack for herself. "He looks good," Angela said.

I picked up a fork and took a bite of potato salad. I sat at the table with my plate and drink. Angela watched me as I slipped another piece of chicken into my mouth. "Why are you staring at me?" I waved my hand in the air.

"I'm trying to figure out when you became me."

I picked up a napkin and wiped my face. "Please don't lecture me again."

"I'm not. But just remember, I have your back—no matter what."

"I hear you, boo."

"Good. Now, focus on getting your business up and going before Granny talks you into moving down here."

"I—"

She held her hand up, cutting me off. "All I'm saying is that she's good at guilting people into doing anything she wants, and you're the prime target since you're single with no kids," Angela reminded me.

I felt like I'd jumped into the dating life too fast after Eric broke my heart. It was at that moment when I found myself at Club Escape with my best friends and bumped into Joseph. From that moment on, we were inseparable. But Joseph was the type of guy that I could only deal with once I was already established with a career and a home, and I was looking to settle down. Once we became an official couple, I decided to quit working under him and pursue my passion full time, so now I was working from home as a graphic designer. I was still in my prime and trying to build up clientele. The sex I had with Joseph was toe-curling insane, but I never saw myself settling down and having kids. We disagreed on where our life paths were going, and I kept feeling like I was moving too fast after being in a long-term relationship, and I needed to be free for a while. So, I stepped back and ended what I had with Joseph, but Eric caught up with me, and I slid back to him—even though he did me dirty in the first place—and now I regretted everything.

"Are you thinking of getting back into the dating pool?" Angela pointed her fork at me, wiggling her eyebrows.

"Nope." I waved her off and sat back in the chair, grabbing my cup and gulping down my drink.

"Don't be like me." Since becoming a wife and

mother, Angela constantly tried to remind us how bad she still was—even with a pregnant belly.

I shrugged, not buying into her words. Yes, I was more into going out now since I'd broken up with Joseph and Eric. But overall, I was still the same person: goal-oriented, a homebody, laid back, and fun.

I felt my phone vibrate. I pushed my plate to the side and pulled my phone out of my pocket.

Dumbass Ex: Hey, can we talk?

Me: No.

Dumbass Ex: I hate that we ended up like this.

Me: That's life. Suck it up.

Dumbass Ex: Jessica, you and I belong together.

Me: Stop texting me!

"When are you going back to New York?"

"My flight is in two days." I placed my phone on the table.

The volume from the living room rose, and I heard laughing and cheering. Granny strolled inside, holding a large margarita with a straw and fanning herself. "Lord, this was so fun," Granny muttered.

"I hope you know this is your Christmas and birthday gift together." Angela stood up and headed to the trash can, scraping her crumbs away. She tossed her plate in the sink. I followed suit.

"Angela, I turned 76 today. I'm not listening to you, child." Granny took a seat while sipping on her margarita.

"How many of those have you had?" I inquired, washing my plate and sticking it in the dishwasher.

"How many men have you slept with today?" she replied.

Angela choked on her water.

I patted her back. "You are a terrible old lady." I chuckled and went to grab a napkin for Angela to clean herself up with.

"You didn't answer the question." Granny placed her drink on the table.

"None."

"Mmm... tell me another one, why don't you?"

"I swear my kids come home with a new word every day from your house," Angela said, glaring at Granny Lynn.

"Angela, find you some business and leave me alone," Granny responded, sticking her tongue out.

Angela and I burst into laughter. "What is wrong with you?" I bent over in laughter, holding my stomach.

"Wrong with who?" Emery asked, coming into the kitchen.

"Your grandmother." Angela pointed her finger at Granny.

"Girl, I can never explain her. Just imagine growing up and having her come to your school," Emery remarked, standing next to us as we stared at Granny, who had her eyes closed and was swaying from side to side in her chair.

"She's a special case, honey," Angela mumbled under her breath.

"Are you staying here tonight, Jessica?" Granny asked.

"Yep."

"You could have stayed at our place," Emery said.

"I didn't want to disturb you and the kids," I said.

"Girl, I need adult company; all the kids do is drive me crazy."

"I would offer my spare room, but Brent and I like to have loud sex," Angela blurted out.

We all groaned in disdain. "Thanks for that reminder," I said.

"Why are you three hiding out in here?" Jackson came into the kitchen with Brent and Joseph behind him.

"Well, look at the time." Angela said and kissed me, Emery, and Granny on the cheek. She headed to Brent, and they locked arms and left.

I blew out a breath, feeling my heartbeat race as Joseph and I stared at each other.

"I just came to check on Granny and say goodbye," Emery answered. Granny waved her off, and Jackson shook his head. He reached for her hand, and they walked out.

"I'm going to bed," I said. I approached Granny with

my arms out for a hug and wished her a happy birthday. Then I turned to face him. "Joseph," I said.

"Jessica." He smiled, slid his hands into his pockets, and leaned to the side to let me walk through the doorway.

The knot that was caught in my throat had my chest on fire. We had not seen each other since I stopped working for him, and then ended our relationship a few months ago. Him being here in town at the same time as I was either a sign, or terrible timing on my part. I wanted him back, but I'd heard he was dating again, and I had no right to interfere in his life.

I made it upstairs to the guest bedroom and shut the door behind me. I blew out a breath. The throbbing between my legs craved his touch, and I needed to soak in a bath and go to sleep. Sex was the last thing I need to be worried about. I grabbed my nightclothes and headed into the bathroom. I turned the shower on, dropped my clothes on the counter, and pinned my hair up. I stared at myself in the mirror. Trying to maintain a career, dating, and family had not hampered my eating habits like I'd thought it would because I'd gained a few extra pounds in my ass and breasts.

Eric, of course, wanted to say something about everything I did when we got back together; that's why I broke up with him. He could not take the rejection and was constantly texting me to get back together. *"Dumbass,"* I whispered to myself and removed my clothes and jumped in the shower to wash off the day and head to bed.

Chapter 2

Jessica

I checked my Apple watch. Seeing it was going on 6 AM, I ran a hand down my face. I needed to get up and dressed to see Brent and spend the day with Emery and Angela. I was there for another day before I would head back home. I had not talked to Scarlett since the day before the party. She wanted to know what was happening with my business and love life. On top of that, my parents had called and wanted to know what I was doing. They'd yelled at me for leaving my good-paying desk job with insurance. Plus, they wondered why I went back to Eric instead of staying with Joseph. But they couldn't see that our personalities were so different. I was more spontaneous, free-spirited, and focused on building my graphic design career. Joseph was the straitlaced, buttoned-up, and dominant type. It had surprised me to see him in a place like Club Escape.

Someone banged on the door. "Jessica! Get up and come down for breakfast."

"I still have half an hour before I need to get up,

Granny!" I called out, tossing the covers back over my head.

"Get up, child; it's not like you got a man in there," Granny spat.

"How do you know?" I questioned, sitting up against the headboard.

"Because the only person getting the D in this house is me. Now, come down for breakfast," Granny Lynn said.

I rolled my eyes, groaned and jumped out of bed. I grabbed my robe and headed to the bathroom to brush my teeth. "Her old ass doesn't know about the D," I mumbled under my breath.

She banged on the door again. "I heard that! You must have forgotten we got thin walls, little girl!" Granny shouted through the door.

"Ugh,This lady here." I blew out a breath and took care of my morning routine.

20 minutes later, I went into the kitchen and saw Pops and Granny, eating breakfast with the TV playing. I smiled and bent down to kiss Pops on the cheek. "Morning, Pops."

"Morning, sweet pea. You sleep well?" He lifted the strawberry jelly and held it out for me.

I picked up a butter knife and toast to fix a sandwich. The table was full of food: pancakes, sausage, eggs, fruit, hash browns, orange juice, and coffee. "Thank you. I did. And what time did everybody leave?" I bit into the toast and moaned, feeling the rumbling of my empty stomach as it got refilled.

"Probably two in the morning." Granny filled her cup of coffee and took a seat across from me at the kitchen table.

"Wow! Did you enjoy yourself?"

She grinned and winked at me.

"Please, Granny, I'm eating." I dropped the toast on my plate and wiped my hands on a napkin. Having to hear about old people's sex lives was not the way to wake up. I shivered in my seat.

"Girl, I tell Angela and Emery all the time—you better pray you can still move like me when you get to be this age." Granny swiveled her hips, lifted her arms in the air, and snapped her fingers.

Pops shook his head, knowing how his wife could be.

I loved their relationship. Growing up in New York and visiting Angela often, I would either be over at their house hanging out or with Emery and Jordan. Now that everyone was married with kids, I didn't get to see them as much and getting in the startup business as an entrepreneur took up a lot of my time.

"How are your brother and your parents?" Pops passed his leftover bacon to Granny, and she piled it on top of her stack of pancakes.

"They're good. My brother's still on the police force, and my parents are still divorced," I joked, checking the time on my watch. I wiped both sides of my mouth and finished drinking my orange juice.

"Make sure you tell them we said hello," he replied.

I nodded, standing and pressing a kiss to each of their cheeks. "I need to head out. I'm meeting Brent, then the girls for lunch."

"Tell them to bring the kids by later!" Granny Lynn yelled.

I walked out of the kitchen and headed out the door toward the rental car. I had been there for a week and did not want to be a burden on them, so I'd rented a car to get around in for a few days. I shut the door and slid the seatbelt on, then typed the address of Brent's office into the navigation center. Right as I backed out of the driveway, my phone rang. I checked the caller ID, and Scarlett's name popped up. "Hey, boo."

"How is L.A.?" she asked.

I looked both ways while turning out of the driveway, then pulled onto the road. They lived in the back of a gated community, away from the other houses. Jackson wanted them to have privacy since their family was well-known in the city. He was a billionaire and owner of a race car team, plus his cousin Arianna was a huge celebrity race car driver. All my friends and family had their shit together, and I was still trying to get my passion off the ground. Everybody tried to offer me money, but I wanted to get to the top on my own. "Good. Ate a lot and slept a lot. Family is good."

"That's good, but you sound weird."

I sighed, trying to decide whether I wanted to mention that Joseph had been there. Finally, I said, "Joseph is here."

"Where? In L.A.?" she asked.

I pulled up to the red light and looked down at the navigation instructions. I forgot to pay attention to the light, and the car behind me honked. I drove off before the light could turn yellow, and I sped up. "He came to the party last night."

"For Granny Lynn?" she queried.

I hopped on the 10 freeway, waiting for the green light, so I could signal to switch lanes. "Yeah, he showed up with Brent."

"I told you it was a bad idea to try again with Eric."

"Scarlett, you and the rest of the world have already

told me how you feel." I let out a frustrated breath at the constant reminders from her and everybody else.

She smacked her lips. "Excuse me for keeping it real."

I got off the freeway and turned left at the light toward Santa Monica. Brent's office was two minutes away, and I planned on heading straight to Emery right after. I turned into the parking structure of Brent's office, parked in the visitors' area, and turned off the ignition. "I have a meeting I need to get to; I'll call you back later."

She grunted and hung up.

I rolled my eyes, not in the mood to deal with her tantrums. I lifted my bag and closed the door, then walked into the building. This was Brent's first advertising business location, and he'd expanded into other cities around the world. He and my cousin had been together ever since college and now, three kids later, it was an amazement since she'd never wanted to get married and have kids. He normally traveled a lot for work, but Angela had told me that since she was less than two months away from giving birth, Brent had decided to stick closer to home.

"Hi, can I help you?" the receptionist asked. She looked to be in her early 30s, like me. She had a short bob, glasses, and golden-brown skin.

"I have an appointment with Brent."

"What's your name?"

"Jessica Samuels."

She typed in my name, wrote it on a visitor badge, and passed it to me. "Here you go. Take that elevator on the right. Floor 15," she said.

I thanked her while taking the name badge and placing it on my shirt. I headed into the corner of the elevator and punched the button for his floor. It was still pretty early, and no one else had stepped on, so I had the elevator to myself. The doors closed, and I saw my reflection in them. I looked like a college student, with my high-waisted jeans and large boyfriend t-shirt. My curls were untamed, and my light makeup showed that I was not in the most glamorous mood.

The elevator dinged, and I got off, seeing that the lobby was quiet, with just his secretary sitting outside. "Hi, Jessica, he's waiting for you."

"Thank you," I repeated and went to tap on his door.

"It's open!" Brent yelled.

I pushed it open and stopped in my tracks. Joseph was sitting in the chair in front of Brent's desk. I cleared my throat and wiped my hands on my pants, feeling nervous suddenly. "I can come back," I said.

"Why? You know Joseph and I have too much going on to reschedule," Brent replied and waved me over.

"Um... okay." I felt sweat beading in my armpits, and my mouth going dry. This was our second time seeing each other in months. I went to go sit on the couch. "Can I have some water, please?" I cleared my throat and looked around the office, avoiding Joseph's piercing stare.

"Is this going to be a problem, Jessica?" Brent stood and headed to the fridge in the corner of his office. He grabbed a bottle of water.

I reached out and grabbed it, twisting the cap off and taking a sip. "What do you mean?"

"Joseph and I are in business together on this project. I hired you, and it slipped my mind about you two," Brent explained.

"Who will I answer to for approval?" I started to remove my sketches from my portfolio.

"Joseph will take lead on this." Brent trudged back over to his chair behind his desk.

My body tensed at the knowledge that Joseph and I would be working closely together. Was this a setup? Were there hidden cameras around? I glanced around his office, then behind the couch, not sure what I would find.

"Jessica, what are you doing?" Brent squinted at me.

"Huh?"

"Why are you lifting the pillows off my couch?"

"I was getting comfortable," I lied, fluffing my hair out. I regretted not putting on more makeup that morning.

"Just like her cousin—crazy," Brent muttered to Joseph, and he chuckled.

"I have a few sketches for you to look at." I stood, stepped over to his desk, and laid them down for him to check over. Brent had hired me to do an overhaul of graphics and logo branding for a real estate company that he'd purchased. His company was doing marketing and advertising in conjunction with my designs. It was a huge project that would set me up to get my company out to the masses. I would always be professional, so working alongside Joseph wouldn't be a problem. However, the hairs on the back of my neck stood up as I felt his presence beside me while we looked over the sketches with Brent.

"These are good, Jess," Brent commented, lifting each logo sample and holding them up together.

"It needs a little more work," Joseph said. "We're going for bold, standout branding for the company." He tapped his finger on the fourth sketch of the two buildings standing next to each other, with Brent's initials over them.

I could not argue, since he was the client, but I made a note to bring it up with Brent later if Joseph was going to have any personal feelings about us working together. "These are samples. Just to get a feel for what ideas you have," I said, moving all four sheets together and putting them back in my binder.

"How much longer will you need to have the final draft?" he asked with a raised brow.

"Normally, it takes me a week or two. I have other clients on top of this one."

"We plan on opening in a month," Joseph announced.

My stomach turned to knots. I desperately wanted to do a good job—not only for myself but to see in his eyes that all the time I'd worked for him while gaining my footing had paid off. Brent was investing a lot in me, and I had Angela to thank for the recommendation. One way or another, I planned on finishing the job and proving to everyone that I was the best designer. I planned on opening my own office one day.

"That's no problem. Who do I need to contact about making the design changes?" I pulled out my phone to take notes.

"Joseph, since you're based in New York," Brent replied. "The company is opening offices in New York and California."

"Does this mean you'll finally buy a place in New York and move my cousin there?" I asked him.

"Not a chance," he joked.

I shook my head and bent to give him a hug, then strode out of the office, not waiting for Joseph to comment. I wondered if he had an inner battle waging inside of himself over whether the two of us working together closely would be a good idea.

As soon as the elevator dinged, I stepped on and hit the L for lobby. I released the long-held breath that I'd been holding as I walked out of the office, swishing my hips. My phone buzzed in my purse, and I lifted it to see that Angela was texting me.

Angela: How did it go?
Me: Great.
Angela: Just great?

I bit my lip, debating whether I should tell her about Joseph right now or wait for lunch.

Me: I will fill you in at lunch.
Angela: Fine but hurry up.
Me: I am 30 minutes away.
Angela: Hurry before I eat without you.

Chapter 3

Jessica

Instead of paying for valet, I parked the car myself at Madre's Restaurant. Traffic was not too terrible from Santa Monica to Echo Park. Plus, listening to Angela complain over the phone nonstop about being hungry made it go faster.

I giggled as I opened the door and saw them all sitting at the table in the middle of the restaurant near the bathrooms, with Angela holding a piece of breadstick to her mouth. "Look who decided to show up," Angela blurted out, rolling her eyes.

"Some of us have to work for a living." I showed off my empty ring finger.

"Because you were stupid and dumped the best guy you ever dated for a hoe." She knew how to push my buttons and bringing up Eric's cheating ass was getting on my last nerve.

"Hi, I'm Madison, I'll be your waitress today." The bubbly, petite blonde waitress placed a menu on the table in front of me, and a glass of water. I picked up the straw and took a sip.

"Our last guest finally arrived," Angela replied. "Can you bring me a bacon cheeseburger, fries, and a milkshake?" Angela leaned back in her chair, rubbing her seven-months-pregnant belly.

"Sounds good," Madison replied. "Anything for you?"

"Can I please have a grilled cheese, fries, and a lemonade?" I closed the menu and passed it to her.

"Oh, can you bring me a grilled cheese, too?" Angela announced.

Madison chuckled at her enthusiasm.

"That's too much, Angela. You're gonna have swollen feet and hands," Emery said, shaking her head.

"I'll be fine. Brent will rub them for me." She shrugged and waved us off.

"You can bring me a grilled cheese and avocado, plus a side salad," Emery said.

"All right, ladies, I'll bring your food out in a few minutes." Madison smiled, gathered our menus, and strolled away.

I looked over at the dessert menu, scanning the pies and cookies they made fresh every day.

"So, tell us how the meeting went," Angela said, lifting her elbow onto the table and putting her palm underneath her chin.

"Joseph was there."

"Oh... what was he doing there?" Angela said.

I rolled my eyes at her fake outrage. "Don't pretend like you didn't set me up, Angela."

"Um, I didn't know he was going to be there," Angela feigned ignorance.

"So, you didn't know they were doing business together?" I squinted at her, searching for any hint of a lie.

"Jessica, we're family; you know me better than that." Angela threw her hands in the air.

"What business are they doing together?" Emery grabbed two sugar packets from the holder and mixed them into her iced tea.

"Real estate," I replied.

"He's doing big things; you should have stayed with him," Angela argued, playing with her nails.

"I don't date men based on how much money they have."

"Oh. We know," Angela joked.

I flipped her off, sucking my teeth.

"I'm still confused about you running back to Eric and dumping Joseph, but we can have that conversation another day," Emery said.

Madison walked over with our food and placed it in front of us. All three of us thanked her, and she left more napkins, and a bottle of ketchup.

"I'm starving," Angela mentioned, picking up her sandwich and smelling it before taking a bite.

"Is this what pregnancy does to you?" I asked.

She mumbled with her mouth full of food, and I laughed at the mustard falling from the side of her lip. "I said, 'My man loves it.'" Angela wiped her mouth with a napkin.

"Do you think this is the last one for you?" I was curious to find out because Brent always wanted a big family, and Angela was late to accept kids—until she called and said she'd found out she was pregnant after a one-night stand with Brent during one of their many breakups.

"Honestly, I tell myself yes, and then I look at my babies and change my mind," Angela explained.

"You've maintained a career, motherhood, and being a wife."

"Yeah, but it's not easy. Brent is a lot of help—and of course, Granny, with her bald-headed ass." Angela laughed at her joke.

Emery threw her napkin at Angela. "Stop talking about my grandmother, or I'll call her." Right as she said that, her phone rang. She picked it up and showed us the name across the screen.

"Speak of the devil," Angela muttered, biting into her burger again.

Emery answered the phone on speaker. "Hey, Granny. What's up?" Emery asked, dipping a French fry in ketchup.

"I felt like somebody was talking about me," Granny Lynn said.

I gasped in shock, covering my mouth.

"Who are you with, Emery?" Granny asked.

Angela waved for her to hang up.

"Angela and Jessica," Emery said.

"Mmm. Tell my baby Jessica hello, but she still owes me rent money," Granny said.

"Granny, I only stayed like two days with you," I blurted out hastily.

"Two days too long," Granny Lynn replied.

"Old lady, is you not going to speak to me?" Angela asked.

"If you put the food down long enough, maybe I will," Granny responded. Emery and I laughed at her statement.

Angela rolled her eyes at us and took a sip of her water. "I'm not even eating," Angela lied, lifting her grilled cheese sandwich.

"You know what the doctor said to you last time. Keep on and see what I do," Granny hinted.

"I'm not scared of you," Angela said.

"I didn't ask you to be scared of me. I can show you better than I can tell you," Granny spat and ended the call.

Angela stared for a few minutes, then looked around the restaurant.

"What are you looking at?" I asked.

"You think she has somebody spying on me?" Angela glanced at the front entrance of the restaurant, then behind her back. The place was crowded with people, so there was no telling if it was true. Ever since Emery kept her lupus diagnosis hidden, the family had become extra strict about keeping up with each other.

"She puts fear in everybody's heart," I said.

"Except Pops," Emery answered.

I nodded, thinking of the two of them, always going back and forth over the littlest thing.

"You and Jackson will turn out like them," Angela said.

"Nope, that's you and Brent. Every other day, you call and complain to me about him, and he calls and complains about you," Emery explained.

Angela's mouth dropped open in surprise. "You're lying," Angela said in shock.

"No, I wish I were. Jackson keeps telling me to block the both of you." Emery took her phone out of Angela's hands and stuck it in her purse.

"I need to write a book on you two and forget about graphic design," I teased.

"Only if you write one on you and Joseph's

mismatched love life, too," Angela taunted, sticking her tongue out at me.

"Whatever, Big Momma."

"When do you fly back to New York?" Emery questioned, pushing her plate forward. Angela snatched up the last of her fries.

"Tomorrow. I have to get back to work on some changes for Brent."

"And your boo," Angela responded.

"Keep eating your food."

"Cousin, you can fool everybody, but I see it in your eyes." She grinned, holding her hands up in surrender.

I pointed one square-shaped fingernail in her face. "Focus on your swollen feet, sis."

Emery looked at the both of us as we glared at each other, then burst into laughter. Our relationship was more than cousins; we were more like sisters.

"Well, let's hope you don't mess this opportunity up," Angela let me know, picking up her ringing phone. "Hey, honey bear," Angela said into the phone.

Honey bear? I mouthed to Emery, and she laughed at me. If that was their special pet name for each other, then it was no wonder she was on Baby #3.

She pursed her lips together, ready to step back to me. I stuffed my mouth with food and pretended to show Emery something on my phone. "Yeah, she's here," Angela said into the phone. "Okay, I'll tell her."

My ears perked up at attention, but she just ended the call and continued eating her food. "What was that about?" I asked.

"Nothing," Angela said with a smirk.

Chapter 4

Jessica

Since departing from lunch with Angela and Emery yesterday, I'd come back to the house and stayed cooped up in the bedroom to finish packing and cleaning before my flight this afternoon. My parents had called me off and on all morning, wondering when I was coming back. Plus, my brother threatened to move into my apartment if I was staying longer because his place was getting renovated. Granny was downstairs cooking, and Pops was watching his afternoon sports game with a beer in his hand. Angela had said she was going to drive me to the airport when she picked up the girls today. They'd spent the night because Brent took Angela out to spend some alone time with her before the baby was born.

I kicked back on the bed and turned the TV up as the door was pushed open, and one the twins ran inside. "Jessi," Marcia said.

I picked her up from the floor and kissed the side of her face as she laughed. My little cousins drove their mom crazy, but I said it was just payback from the way she acted when she was younger. "What are you doing up here, little girl?" I tickled her and kissed all over her face.

"I dunno." Her little one-and-a-half-year-old self was the opposite of her sister. We thought she got it from Granny because she got into everything. Anytime we had something in our hands—from food to a piece of paper—she was snooping to get it into hers.

"Marcia, where are you, little girl?!" I heard Granny Lynn yell through the hallway. Marcia tried to hide behind me. Granny pushed the door open and shook her head at Marcia's little butt sticking up in the air. "Somebody is trying to hide from me." Granny shuffled into the room, wearing her usual housecoat, with her hair in a bun on top of her head.

"You going to bingo tonight?" I questioned, turning to lift Marcia up in my arms.

She giggled at Granny, who was holding a towel in her hand. She bent down and wiped Marcia's face and hands with it, then tossed it on top of the desk in the room. "No, staying home to make sure you get off with no issues."

"I'll be fine, Granny. My flight leaves in three hours. Go have fun."

"I can go to bingo anytime. Plus, I'm watching the girls for Angela and Brent."

"Where did Brent take her this time?"

"Some couples' spa." She took a seat on the edge of the bed.

I passed the remote to Marcia, who kept clicking through different channels. "Angela needs to relax. She only has two months left."

"I keep telling her that, but she doesn't listen."

Angela worked at the salon at all hours or took the

girls around town and pampered them throughout the day. All three of them were spoiled by Brent, but lately he took it up a notch because she was pregnant and thinking about going back to work right away. He wanted her to take at least a year or two off to focus on the kids and him.

"Angela's your twin," I said. "Even though she's not related to you by blood, she still has your personality."

"You take after me, too. Don't act like you're some innocent victim."

I faked being offended, putting my hand on my chest. "Granny, I have no idea what you're talking about."

"Sure, Freckles."

Getting up from the bed, I kissed Marcia on the cheek, and then Granny. I went to the bathroom to clean up before heading to the kitchen.

"Give that boy a chance," she said.

I washed my hands and dried them off. "I'm focused on my business right now; besides, he hates me."

"What makes you think he hates you?"

Honestly, ever since Eric broke my heart, I had been on a "fuck feelings" type of vibe. I knew I was stupid to go back to him and entertain the possibility of a relationship. Call me naive or dumb, but I needed closure and to know that I was not the reason for the breakup originally. He had issues because I was a good girlfriend, and unfortunately Joseph only got little pieces of me. I hoped we could be friends going forward, and that he'd find someone who would appreciate the man that he was. "What did you cook?" I asked, changing the subject. I strolled out of the bathroom and followed her downstairs.

Marcia grabbed her hand and walked in front of me with her bow-legged, chubby legs. Her curly hair was up in big pigtails that dangled back and forth.

"Good try on changing the subject," Granny said. "I'll let you get away with it for now."

We made it downstairs, and I flopped down on the couch next to Pops, while she went to the kitchen. Marcia tried to climb up onto the couch, and Pops bent over to help her up. "Pops!" Marcia squealed, clapping her hands.

"Pretty girl. You sleepy?" Pops asked her. She buried her head against his neck.

"She's been running around here all day," I said. "Where's Jazmine?"

"In their room, asleep," Pops said.

I forgot they had a bedroom at the house. They even had one at Emery's for whenever they spent the night there. The bond between all three of them was beautiful. I sometimes thought about moving there to be closer to them and have the same type of friendship, but I loved living in New York.

"What's up with you? I know that boy got your mind wandering," Pops said.

I groaned, not wanting to get another opinion on my love life for the second time in a day. "Just working and focusing on my career, Pops."

"Aren't you out of a job?" Pops asked.

"What? No. Who told you that?" I crinkled my brows in shock.

"My wife said you can barely pay the bills since you broke that boy's heart, and he fired you. She wanted to start up a collection plate for you at the church," Pops said.

I buried my head in my hands. That old woman got into everybody's business except her own. "Pops, I'm fine. I promise."

"You sure? I can give you a few dollars to hold you over until you get another job," he said.

I bent over in laughter. He looked at me with raised brows. I waved a hand at him. "That wife of yours needs to mind her business. Let's go eat, so I can get on my flight later." I jumped up and grabbed Marcia out of his arms, then helped him stand. He didn't need his cane all the time but kept it by him in case he got tired.

The kitchen was bumping with old-school '60s R&B music, and Granny was humming to herself. I put Marcia in the highchair and grabbed a sippy cup for her, then rolled up my sleeves to help Granny get lunch prepared.

"Baby, why did you say Jessica was out of work?" He broke the peace and quiet that I was hoping to have until I left for the airport.

"What are you talking about?" Granny asked, turned the heat down on the stove. She glanced over at him as he stood in front of the fridge.

"Jessica said she didn't get fired," Pops mentioned, opening the fridge and grabbing a beer. He sat at the head of the kitchen table.

"I didn't say she was fired. I said she was stupid for dumping her sexy boss for Eric's lazy tail." Granny pursed her lips together, daring me to respond. She loved to get under my skin and debate back and forth with me.

"I'm not involved," I said, lifting the cornbread from the top of the stove and placing it on the table.

"Well, what do you plan on doing for money? How do your parents feel about it?" Pops investigated.

I gritted my teeth, ready to end this conversation. "My parents haven't paid my bills in over 15 years, Pops. I'm working on my graphic design business."

"What's a graphic design?" he asked, breaking a piece of cornbread off and feeding it to Marcia.

"Hello, party people," Angela said, walking into the kitchen and holding Jazmine in her arms. She was wiping her eyes from sleep, while Angela rubbed her back.

"Didn't I tell you about sneaking into my house?" Granny asked.

"I have a key, old woman," Angela replied.

"For emergencies, and this ain't an emergency. What if my husband and I were congregating?" Granny asked.

Angela and I looked at each other, shaking our heads. "Please keep that to yourself," Angela answered, sitting next to me.

"You better remember what I tell you: A happy husband equals a happy wife. Don't hurt to get on your knees once every blue moon," Granny announced.

I started to gag.

"Can you not talk about your sex life in front of my children, please?" Angela covered Jazmine's ears in horror.

"Girl, they don't understand what I'm saying. I talked to you and Emery about sex when y'all were around 11."

"And?" Angela shrugged.

"How about 'you're welcome'? I should be charging and become a sex therapist for couples," Granny taunted. She kissed Pops on the lips, and he winked at us.

I dropped my napkin on the table and stood. "Angela, take me to the airport, please."

"I thought you were hungry?" Granny asked.

I looked down at my watch, then back up at them. "Sorry, can't miss my flight," I lied. "Thanks again, Granny and Pops." I was ready to get out of that house and back to my home, away from the horny old couple. I raced upstairs and grabbed my bags and purse, then came back downstairs to meet Angela at the door. "Thanks," I told her.

"No worries. I'm used to their nasty asses," Angela said.

* * *

40 minutes later, we pulled up to LAX, and I jumped out of the car and grabbed my luggage from the backseat. I bent down to the car window to say goodbye.

"Call me when you make it, Jess," Angela said.

"I will. And keep me updated on Little Man," I replied. I tapped the top of the car and walked inside the airport.

It was not too crowded for a Thursday afternoon, so I breezed through check-in and removed my shoes and belt to stand in line for the body scanner. A few minutes went by as they checked my ID, then I headed to my terminal. My stomach grumbled, so I stopped at Subway and grabbed a 6" veggie sub and drink as the plane started to board. The flight was overbooked, but I hoped to get a nice middle or aisle seat near the back in case I needed to get to the bathroom and ended up sitting next to someone who hated to let people get up.

"*Boarding First Class, A-E,*" the check-in counter attendant said over the loudspeaker.

I moved fast to catch up with the line, tossing my sandwich in my purse. I held onto my luggage and let them scan my ticket. I followed a woman with her two kids and prayed I didn't have a seat near them, and that the flight would not be long.

"Welcome aboard," the flight attendant said.

I nodded, walking down the crowded aisle, as passengers put their luggage away. I looked down at my ticket, then back up at the seat labels, and I found that I was sitting in the perfect middle spot. Then my smile dropped when I saw the person sitting next to me was none other than Joseph.

"Excuse me, can I get by?" a guy said from behind me.

"Um... sorry." I dropped my carry-on bag onto the aisle seat and squeezed in, so he could get by.

Joseph removed the headphones from his ears and looked up at me. "Hey," Joseph said.

"What are you doing here?" I questioned, pushing my bags into the overhead compartment.

"Going home, like you," he joked.

I cursed at myself for asking a stupid question. I sat down in the middle seat and buckled up, pushing my hair behind my ears and trying not to appear so nervous—even though my palms were sweating, my throat was dry, and my stomach growling from not eating earlier at Granny's place. "I know—stupid question."

He licked his lips and nodded.

"Granny was surprised you came to her party," I continued.

"I like Emery's grandparents. Plus, Brent and I go way back."

The flight attendant got on the overhead speaker and called for everyone to take a seat, then gave instructions. I got as comfortable as possible before an older woman came in at the last minute and pushed her bags into the overhead compartment, then sat next to me. She was probably around 50 or 60 years old. She plopped down and pulled out a magazine, her glasses, and some snacks from her purse. "Hello, would you like some?" She held a bag of peanuts toward us.

"No, thank you," I replied.

She shrugged.

"We will be in California in six hours and 20 minutes. Please turn off all cell phones before liftoff," a flight attendant said over the loudspeaker.

"Aren't you an actress?" the other flight attendant asked.

"No," I replied, chuckling. I peered over at Joseph, who was staring out the window, then down at his phone in his hands. He started to turn it off when a message popped up with a woman's name on it.

"Can I get you all anything to drink?"

I was startled out of my staring by the attendant with the drink cart next to us.

"I'll take a Pepsi, please," the older woman said.

"Sure. Anything for you two?" The flight attendant smiled wide at Joseph, and a part of me felt jealous.

"I'll take a bottle of water," Joseph replied.

"Anything else I can get you? I want to make sure your flight is smooth," the flight attendant flirted right in my face. She bent over, trying to show off her cleavage that barely was covered in her tight vest. She didn't even know if we were there together, and she was letting it be obvious that she was available to fuck. "You need anything?" She arched an eyebrow at me, finally giving me attention.

"Water." I did not want to think she rolled her eyes at me, but the way she tossed the bottle and hurried to the next seat was convincing.

"Well, she doesn't like you," the older woman said.

"Excuse me?"

"I'm Belinda. What's your name?" she asked, extending a hand for a shake.

"Jessica."

"Watch out for that one, because she's after your man." Belinda said, pointing at Joseph.

He choked on his water. I patted him on the back, and Belinda passed him a napkin. "We're not together," he said quickly.

"You sure? I can tell from a mile away that you two look good together," Belinda replied.

"I'm single and not looking for a man," I said.

"Don't block your blessing, honey," Belinda remarked.

The plane steadied. I closed my eyes and put my air pods in to block out the nonsense around me. I drifted off to sleep, thinking of the last time I was happy in a relationship, and the only thing that I could think of was Joseph and I at a dinner date.

* * *

"What are you doing?" I questioned, watching him pull off his jacket and place it on the park bench. We'd just come from dinner at my favorite restaurant to celebrate another closed deal for him.

"Come here." He reached out for my hand.

I placed it into his palm, and he pulled me close and kissed the side of my neck. He buried his face between my shoulder and neck and squeezed my ass. "Are you being spontaneous right now?" I pulled back from him, stopping him from sucking on my neck, so I could stare into his eyes.

"You say I never live for the moment. Well, here we are." He lifted me up and placed me on top of the bench

with my butt on his jacket. He stepped between my legs and pushed my skirt up.

"Joseph, are you serious?"

He cut me off with a kiss, sliding my panties to the side. "Very serious," he responded.

I squeezed my eyes shut tight, not caring if anyone saw us. I lifted my hands around his neck and pulled him in closer. "Mmm."

Chapter 5

Joseph

The party was the first time I had seen Jessica since she broke up with me a few months ago. From what Brent said, she was not fooling with her ex anymore, either, and he thought I should give it another shot. But I was at a point where I would no longer put my heart on the line for any woman only to end up with more drama and a broken heart. I wanted what my parents had, and I figured Jessica would be the one to give me that everlasting love, but she wanted to focus on working things out with her ex instead. I could admit that I was used to being spoiled, and the center of attention with both my parents and the women I dated, but I would give the same attention back to Jessica if she chose to be my girl. My parents, Joseph Sr. and Marion, had showed me that true love was possible if I worked toward it.

Now, my focus was on building my businesses with the detailing shops I'd opened across New York and California, plus the real estate business that I was starting soon with Brent. I was looking into more opportunities to grow my portfolio.

It was funny to me, how Jessica showed a little jealousy in her eyes when the flight attendant was flirting with me. Someone who had broken up with me to go back to her ex shouldn't have been up in arms about who I dated.

"Mmm…" Jessica moaned, and my dick jerked in my pants.

The lights turned on, and we prepared to land. "Please push all trays forward and buckle your seats," the flight attendant said over the speaker.

Jessica's head leaned against my shoulder; her hair fell across her face. I pushed it back behind her ear.

"Any trash?" The attendant who had brought our drinks earlier started picking up trash from each person.

Jessica woke, startled, with a little drool running down her lip. I smirked as she looked around to see if anyone was looking.

"Girl, that dream must have been good," Belinda said. I chortled, knowing what was coming next.

"Huh?" Jessica replied.

"You must have had a nice dream, from the moans coming out of your mouth," Belinda said.

Jessica gasped in shock. "I don't know what you're talking about." Jessica hurriedly lifted her blanket and stood when the plane landed.

Belinda smirked and stood to let her out. I sat back, watching how she would get out of this situation. "Nothing wrong with a sex dream; I still have a few myself," Belinda commented.

"I wasn't having a sex dream," Jessica spat, grabbed her luggage from up top while rolling her eyes. She headed down the aisle toward the door.

I shook my head and stood, gathering my things.

"She likes you," Belinda said.

"What makes you think that?"

"No one gets that upset over a dream." Belinda winked at me and passed me my backpack.

I tossed it over my shoulder and let her pass through first before heading off the plane and out of the terminal to the transportation area. I made it down in front of the shared rides and saw Jessica loading her bags into a minibus. "You have any more space?" I asked the driver. He nodded, and I threw my bags to him and held the door open to let Jessica in first. "Ladies first."

"Thanks," she mumbled and jumped into the bus.

I went to the same aisle as her. It was full to capacity, so we sat in the back as the driver closed the doors and locked in our address.

"Here we go, everybody," the driver said, turning the music low, while he drove out of the airport terminal.

I turned my phone back on and saw missed calls and messages from my family, friends, and Natasha, a girl that I had hung out with a few times during the past few months. I'd met her at Club Escape, and we'd played together a few times, but I didn't take it seriously outside the club.

"Date waiting?" Jessica asked.

I lifted my eyes to meet hers. "What are you talking about?"

"Your phone's blowing up. Some girls must have missed you."

I ran a hand down my face, licking my lips and wondering whether I should carry on this conversation with her. Honestly, she was the one who broke things off with me, and now she was questioning me about who was blowing up my phone. "Something like that."

"Is it someone from the club?" she questioned.

The bus stopped and let off the two girls who sat in the second row. The driver helped them out and opened the back door to get their luggage.

"Would it matter?" I asked.

She jerked back at my response. "Whatever."

I groaned, feeling myself get heated at the direction of this conversation. I'd said to her the first time that if she was not ready for a relationship, then she should let me know, but the minute I stuck my dick inside her, it was over for her dating anyone else. Now, the second things ended between us, she thought she could question me about who I was dating. "How's Eric?" I asked.

Jessica sucked her teeth and glared at me, scooting closer to the window. "You know what..." She chuckled in annoyance.

"So, you can question me, but I can't ask you about your ex?"

"Totally different situations," Jessica mentioned.

I just about popped my neck, turning to look at her. "Whatever, Jess."

"Yeah, whatever." she mumbled under her breath.

"Are you trying to get the last word here?" I teased, watching her squirm in her seat.

"I don't need the last word, Joseph."

I snorted and checked a text message from my father.

Dad: Your mother wants you to come to dinner tomorrow.

Me: That's cool. I am back in town.

Dad: How was the party?

Me: Pops and Granny doing good.

"4538 Brand Park," the driver announced, pulling in front of my condo.

I slid my phone into my pocket and looked over at Jessica as the driver opened the back door to grab my bags. She stared back at me.

"This is what you wanted," I reminded her.

Jessica gasped in shock with her mouth wide open.

"Here you go," the driver said.

I pulled out my wallet, stepped out of the bus, and gave him a $20 tip. He walked around and shut the door. I watched Jessica inside the bus, peering back at me and rolling her eyes. The shuttle pulled away, and I turned to walk inside my building and up to my place.

"Hey, Joseph," the receptionist said. I'd gotten her this job a year ago, before I met Jessica. She was a single mom with two kids, and she'd come into my father's shop with her car broken down. He told me about her, and I helped her out by setting her up with a receptionist position at my building.

"What's up, Lira?" I went through the mail that she passed me on the desk. I started to walk to the elevator.

"Wait!" Lira ran around the desk and met me at the elevator.

"What's up?" I sighed, exhausted from what had happened with Jessica.

She passed me some papers, and I looked down to see it was for a cookie sale with her son's name it. I chuckled and leaned against the open door. "I wanted to see if I you could help me out and purchase some boxes." Lira held a pen out for me to take.

I signed my name, put down an order for 10 boxes, and passed it back. "Of course, anything for Little Man. Good seeing you," I said. I stepped onto the elevator and hit the 10th floor. Lira waved at me, and I gave her a thumbs up.

I got off, heading to my door. I opened the door and dropped my bags near the couch, along with my keys and wallet. I pressed the button on my answering machine and walked to the kitchen to see if my mom had left me any food for the week.

"Mr. Michaels, please get back to us at your earliest convenience about the center," I heard a message play.

I popped the top on the beer bottle and went to play it back.

"Mr. Michaels, please get back to us at your earliest convenience about the center."

On top of my businesses, I had plans to open a community center for low-income families. My cousins— and surprisingly, Jessica's brother—were working with me on building the center for the neighborhood. I had the money, but I wanted to get a huge sponsor to come in to support us and give a donation for computers, sports equipment, and furniture. I could have purchased it all right out of the gate, but I wanted to see businesses come in and help build it back up.

The next message played. *"Yo! Bro, call me back when*

you're home, so we can make plans." My cousin—really, more like a brother—Rory Michaels was a coach at a local high school, and the biggest hoe in the world. He loved women, and women loved him, and that caused me problems because they all thought I could get him to grow up and commit to them.

I decide to order some food, and then call him back before showering and watching a movie. I logged into UberEATS to get food from one of my favorite restaurants around the corner. Since it was not too late, I got a steak-and-cheese sandwich with fries. Finally, after setting up my order, I dialed Rory back.

"Yo! Your old ass made it home safe?" Rory joked.

"Fuck you, Rory," I grunted, looking for my remote on the coffee table that had been cleaned off. I had a maid service come once a week to keep the place clean. I was a true bachelor with a two-bedroom, three-bathroom condo. It had a fireplace and a 70" TV. The kitchen was separate, and I had my master suite upstairs, and a guest bedroom downstairs. I had all the amenities in my building, like a gym, media center, and rooftop for parties. One thing I didn't do was bring women here. I liked to meet at a hotel, or their place, so they wouldn't get the wrong idea. The only woman besides my mom who had seen the place was Jessica.

"Don't tell me you're thinking about her again," Rory blurted out.

I changed the channel to a local ball game. "Who?"

"Your future wife, Jessica." Rory joked.

I wanted to punch him in the face for bringing up her name. I had been doing good, not thinking about her for the rest of the night, and now he started up. "What time are we meeting up for the game?" I asked, changing the subject.

I heard snickering on the other end of the call. "Look at you, trying to not think about Freckles," Rory continued, joking around.

"At least I can bring her home to my mom. Your girl is trying to run you over because you can't keep your dick in your pants," I taunted, laughing at him going off on me.

"Man, fuck you, Joseph. Leave that crazy girl out of this."

"You should have left Scarlett alone a long time ago. Now, she's showing up at your job and trying to become your wife," I teased, shaking my head at him. I'd met Scarlett through Rory, and the other friends she used to mess with. I didn't really care for her high-maintenance attitude, but she was Jessica's friend, and Rory's sometimes-girlfriend when they were not fighting back and forth.

The phone notification popped up for my food arrival, and I told Rory I would see him this weekend, then ended the call. I jumped up and answered the door, grabbing my food and tipping the driver a 20. I went back to the couch to eat and watch the game. I didn't plan on going back out for the rest of the night since I needed to check on my business tomorrow, and then meet with some more businesses about donating.

After I scarfed down the food, I jumped in the shower and let the hot water cascade down my back as I thought about Jessica's face in the van earlier today. She didn't like people pointing out her freckles, but I loved kissing each one and tracing my tongue down her long, sexy neck that curved up to her pillowy lips and oval-shaped eyes.

"Fuck!" I could feel my dick standing at attention as I

thought about her. I rubbed out the ache and turned the shower off. I snatched a towel and dried off before getting into bed and setting my alarm for another early day at the office.

Chapter 6

Joseph

The day started off good with my morning coffee from the shop around the corner that I frequented, and then I grabbed some donuts for the office. I stepped out of the car and headed inside my building. Some people would say that I only ran a detail shop for cars, so I shouldn't have to wear a suit, but I prided myself on being a businessman at all times and preparing for any opportunity that could potentially present itself, so wearing a suit represented my brand at all times.

I open the door to a busy office, with clients sitting around, waiting to be seen. I nodded at the two guys talking with Terry, one of my shop designers.

Since Jessica left, I'd hired Patty, an older woman who was more like an aunt to me. She always complained that I needed to find a good woman and settle down. "What did you bring me?" Patty asked, hanging up the phone.

I placed the box of donuts on her desk. "Donuts."

"You know I'm trying to lose weight, Joseph," Patty

fussed, opening the box of donuts. She picked out a strawberry frosted, bit into it, and closed her eyes, moaning.

I titled my head and stared at her, waiting to see when she would open her eyes again, then I cleared my throat.

"What?" she asked.

"I thought you were trying to lose weight." I laughed.

She stuck her hand out, waving me off. Patty followed me into my office, still eating her donut. I took a seat at my desk and checked my messages. "How was the trip?" Patty asked, taking a seat in the chair next to my desk.

"Fine." I typed in my password to check my emails and calendar. Before I left, I'd pushed a lot of appointments back to go to California for the party.

"That's all it was? Fine?"

I stopped typing and leaned back in my chair. I stared at Patty. "I saw her."

"Jessica?"

I nodded, releasing a long-held breath. "Yep."

"What was that conversation like?"

I crossed my arms over my chest. "We didn't talk, really, besides a hi and bye."

"Why are you being so stubborn?" Patty pushed her lips forward in a pout.

"Shouldn't you be taking client information?" I hated how she knew me just as well as my parents and called me out on my bullshit. I was the one who had been wronged in the relationship, not Jessica.

"You act like the girl ran over your dog or something."

"That equals breaking my heart in some circles, Patty."

"Then be the respectable man who I know your mother raised and talk to each other like adults."

"Who do I have for my first appointment?"

Patty got up from the chair and left my office without answering.

I continued looking over my upcoming appointments. Some people wanted the basic package, and others wanted the full package with color and design. The business had been recently showcased in the local paper for small businesses that keep growing without huge backing. I'd made it my business to invest and market in my area and local towns in New York.

There was a knock at the door.

"Come in," I said without looking.

Natasha stepped inside, smiling and holding two cups of coffee. "Hey," she said, putting the coffee down on my desk in front of me.

"What are you doing here?" I asked.

"I wanted to see you. It's been a while, and I thought since you're back, we could do dinner." Natasha was a beautiful woman with flawless, hazel-brown skin, slender hips, and a nice, round ass, but I liked my women with a little more meat on their bones. Natasha worked as a realtor, and she sometimes helped out at the local schools when they were shorthanded.

"I have back-to-back meetings today."

She fidgeted with her hands and looked around the room, not making eye contact.

I grinned. Sometimes, when we were at the club, I liked her shyness, but today I needed her to speak up.

"Can we have lunch, at least?" Natasha held her breath, waiting for an answer.

I felt a twinge of guilt for not giving her as much attention as she would have liked outside the club, but I was not in the mindset of committing to anybody. I checked the time on my watch, and my schedule. "I'm sorry, Natasha. I have back-to-back meetings, but I'll call you."

She rolled her eyes and started to speak when my phone rang. I picked it up, glad for the distraction.

"Mr. Michaels, this is Jack Foster from Tech Regional," said the voice on the other end.

"Mr. Foster, good to hear from you again." I opened my desk drawer and pulled out the file on Tech Regional, a local company that installed computers in schools around the world. Rory had told me about them, and I'd decided to reach out and see if we could collaborate for the community center.

"I was checking in about meeting up to discuss the center and a donation," Jack said.

"Today would be perfect. I have one meeting with a designer for the grand opening."

"That would be great if two o'clock could work," Jack explained. There was a muffled sound on the other end.

"Two o'clock can work." I was planning on meeting with Taylor later, but I could move her up earlier. I finished the call and hung up, having forgotten that I was not alone. "Listen, Natasha—"

She held up a hand, stopping me. "Look, I like you, Joseph, and I think we hit it off a few times, and we could be good together."

"Sorry, but I don't feel the same way. You'll meet someone that brings out the same feelings, but it's not me."

"But we had such good times at the club," Natasha argued.

I agreed, in a sense. "Yeah, at the club, but I need more than that type of environment for a relationship."

"We could try. We could start by going to lunch

together." Natasha walked around my desk and slid between my legs.

The door opened, and Patty just walked inside without knocking. "Sorry to interrupt," Patty said, glaring at Natasha. They did not like each other at all, and Patty did not have a problem telling her to her face that she was just a plaything until Jessica came back.

"We're busy. Don't you know how to knock?" Natasha hissed, putting her hands on her hips. Her brows dipped low in frustration.

"If it were important, I *would* have knocked. But seeing as Joseph doesn't look too thrilled to see you, then I guess it isn't," Patty replied.

Natasha glanced over at me, and I lifted my arms in a shrug. I scooted back, and Natasha went to grab her purse and coffee, getting ready to leave. "This isn't over, Joseph. We need to talk." Natasha rushed out of the office, bumping Patty in the shoulder.

"I changed my mind. I'm *not* sorry to interrupt." Patty grinned mischievously.

"Huh?"

"Are you listening to me?"

I did not have the heart to tell her that I'd tuned her out. I picked some papers up off my desk, released a breath, and rubbed a hand over my hair, shifting in my office chair. "What do you need, Patty?"

"I want you to connect with Willy about the Benz paint job because it's still not done," Patty said.

It was not in me today to get on Willy about keeping his timeframe on track. He was a grown man, and I paid all my workers a great paycheck. "What's the problem with the Benz paint job?"

"It should have been done two days ago, and the

owner is calling again. I'm tired of them goofing off and not being on time—"

I cut her off. "I'll handle it, Patty."

"Good. Now, if you'll excuse me, I have some new clients to input into the database," Patty said cheerfully and walked off.

I reached over and typed in the information for the Benz 2021 account, then pulled up the name and specifications of what was supposed to be done and when. The customer wanted tinted windows, cream-colored designs, and installation. We did more than just detailing; we made a huge name for ourselves as the go-to company for any and everything design-related for your car.

I printed out the information and stood, heading to the shop to see if Willy was there. I had 10 employees at this location, 12 at my Brooklyn location, and 20 in my California location since it was a two-story standalone building. I heard laughing and yelling from the other side of the door, and I pushed it open.

Denver, Big Rob, and Willy were huddled together, laughing. Denver was the shop manager, while Rob and Willy were expert designers. "Look what the cat dragged in." Denver pushed his hand out for a shake.

I dapped him with a closed fist. "Y'all back here working or gossiping?" I waved around the room, with three cars on the landing belt, waiting to be serviced.

"Here he goes." Rob tittered like a 12-year-old kid.

I flipped him off. "What's on the agenda today?" I leveled a look at him, waiting for an answer. He knew I would get irritated if I had to constantly wait for an answer to a simple question. Willy's eyes shifted toward me. "What's up with the Benz detailing setup?" I flipped through the clipboard on the wall.

"I'm almost done with it." Willy lifted the spray cord to prepare to paint the Benz.

"Cool."

"We only have these three today," Denver confirmed, taking the clipboard off the wall and walking around to the desk in the corner.

"Rory said we're balling tomorrow at 1 PM. Are you good with that time?" I asked, watching Willy paint a straight line across the side of the Benz.

"Yep. He still owes me 50 bucks from the last game," Denver complained and looked up at me.

"Take that up with him. I'm heading out for another meeting. Call me if you need me." I turned to leave.

They all yelled out at the same time, "All right!"

* * *

I parked in the small structure outside the business district, close to the Bronx library. I got out of the car and hit the alarm on my Lexus, then removed my shades as I walked inside Taylor Made Designs. The place was a nice size, with a visiting area, a coffee machine, a few offices, and a conference room. I was thinking of opening a business in the same building since it had high foot traffic.

I'd found Taylor through my mom's bake shop; she'd used her for an event last year. This was my first time using her for a huge job like this, and I needed to make sure that we were on the same page.

"Joseph! How are you?" Taylor's high-spirited voice rumbled through the room as she stepped out of her office with a file in her hand. She was shorter than me—at least 5'4" or 5'5"—with wide hips, full breasts, and a fat ass. Many times, I noticed her flirting with me, but I ignored it since I didn't mix business with pleasure after past situations. She leaned over and wrapped her arms around my shoulders for a hug. That had thrown me off the first time we met, but she'd said she was a hugger. I still didn't know whether that was true or not.

"I'm good, Taylor. Thanks for meeting with me now."

"We can go into my office. My assistant ran out to grab some lunch." Taylor reached for the door handle and pushed it farther open to let me inside.

I took a seat in the chair at her desk. "So, I sent the check for the center."

Taylor fiddled with some papers on her desk. I stared at her office walls. She had plaques from her time in school at Spelman University, family photos, and pictures taken at major events with high-profile celebrities. "Yes. I have the receipt here, and all the deposits have been paid," Taylor said.

"Hopefully, more sponsors will come onboard."

"That would be great, Joseph. I have the color scheme mapped out in gold and black." Taylor turned her computer to show me the digital layout of the center's celebration—a banner with the company name, and balloons with drapes hanging around.

"My parents have a 35th anniversary party right after the center opens."

"You need me to design that, as well?" Taylor asked.

"If you're free to handle back-to-back events."

"I am; don't worry." Taylor smirked.

I peeled my eyes away and cleared my throat. "Since that's confirmed, I need to get out of here before I'm late for my next meeting." I stood.

"Wait!" Taylor reached over her desk and grabbed my

wrist. I looked down, then back up at her. "Sorry." She released me.

I slid my hands into my pockets. "What is it? If it's about the cost, don't worry. Money is no object for my parents."

She closed her eyes briefly in thought. "Um, I don't know how to go about this."

"Go about what?"

"Would you be interested in going out to dinner with me?" Taylor whispered.

I felt my body tense up at her question. I was already dealing with Natasha wanting to date me. Now, Taylor? Something told me this was going to blow up in my face if I did not tread lightly, since she had just agreed to do my parents' anniversary party. "Taylor, you're a beautiful woman."

"But not beautiful enough for you. I get it." Taylor sat back down at her desk.

"That's not what I said."

"You can be honest. I'm a big girl." Taylor laced her fingers in front of her on the desk.

"It's complicated."

"There's someone else?" She scrunched her eyebrows together in confusion.

Thinking about Jessica from the other night, I could not say whether things were really finished. Like Brent said: *There comes a point where you will lose her for good if you don't forgive her.* "No," I replied.

"Then if it's not someone else—"

"I don't mix business with pleasure, Taylor. I did that in the past, and it didn't work out."

"But I'm not her." Taylor watched the hesitation in my eyes.

"Still. It wouldn't be right when I have too much going on with my businesses and trying to balance a dating life."

"I'll take it as a challenge and prove you wrong." Taylor cocked her head to the side and winked.

I laughed and walked out of her office as her assistant was bringing her lunch in. I jumped in my car and backed out onto the road, so I could head over to Tech Regional before they closed. My phone rang, and I turned it on speaker since I was driving.

"Hello." I heard a soft voice come through the phone.

"Jessica?" I asked, checking the number to make sure I was not confused.

"It's me." Jessica sounded unsure—even scared.

"Why are you calling me?" I didn't mean to sound harsh, but we hadn't held a conversation in months—other than on the flight back. Even at Granny's party, we'd put distance between us.

"I have something of yours, and I wanted to see when we could meet again to discuss the design job."

"What do you have?" I stopped at a red light.

"One of your bags was mixed up with mine, and I didn't know until I got home," Jessica explained.

My brows dipped in confusion. "Okay. I'm about to head to a meeting. I can pick it up tomorrow."

"I can drop it off to you this evening."

"I have dinner plans."

Silence came through the phone. I could have told her it was with my parents, but she hadn't earned that privilege from me.

She made a disapproving sound. "You can tell your little girlfriend I'm not trying to ruin your date," Jessica said.

I exhaled and chortled at the little hint of jealousy in her tone. "Like I said, I have plans, so I'll pick it up later."

"What about the design logo?" Jessica asked.

"I can see it when I come to pick up the bag."

"I can meet you in your office, Joseph."

I groaned, getting more annoyed at her push back. "Jessica, what do you think is going to happen? We've been over, and I'm not looking to go backwards."

"That makes two of us," she spat, and I heard the dial tone.

"Women."

30 minutes later, I made it to Tech Regional. I left my keys with a valet and went inside to greet the owner and finally get the ball rolling on the computer donation.

* * *

Later that evening, I was feeling high after closing the deal with Tech Regional, and I grabbed a bottle of wine and a bottle of scotch to celebrate with my parents.

I used to pop in to surprise them, but I learned early on to stop. They would often be in the middle of things that no child should ever have to see.

I knocked at the door, and it swung open to reveal my mom's beautiful smile. "My baby!" Mom stood on her tiptoes and hugged me around the neck, almost suffocating me.

I chuckled and patted her on the back soothingly. "Mom, I can't breathe."

She let me go and smacked me lightly on the chest. "Boy, please, you know you miss me," Mom said.

"Did you do something to your hair?"

"You like it? I had the girl at the local shop color it and

ring-curl it." She stood to the side and let me stroll in as my father came to greet me.

"I do, but you're always beautiful. Old man, how are you feeling?"

"Boy, stop filling your momma's head up, now. She already thinks she's Cardi B."

"Pop!" I groaned, not wanting to hear him talk about my mother that way. I shoved the bottles toward my mom and removed my jacket to sit on the couch next to him.

"I made your favorites, baby," she said, kissing me atop my head. She went back into the kitchen.

"Great because I'm starving." I rubbed my hands together.

"You had all day to eat, son," Dad informed me, turning the volume up on the TV. The football game was on.

I leaned my hand on the back of the couch, getting ready for a long conversation about what I should be doing with my personal business. "Not today, please."

"Did you get the business worked out with Brent?" Dad asked, taking a glass of scotch out of my mom's hands.

She passed the second one to me, and I took a sip and sighed, feeling fully relaxed. "Yep. Brent and I looked at the blueprints, and the designs are coming together for the opening."

"What about the community center?" he queried.

"I met with an event designer today and set every-thing up."

"He's using Taylor, honey!" Mom called from the kitchen. "The girl who planned the bakery shop events!"

"Is she cute?" Dad wondered.

"Yeah."

"Yeah? What's wrong with her?"

"Nothing. She's sweet and cool, I guess."

"Come and eat, you two!" Mom yelled.

The both of us stood and went to the kitchen. We sat at the table. "Talk some sense into your son, Marion," Dad fussed, picking up a plate of fried catfish and placing two strips on his plate.

My mom felt the top of my forehead, like I was a little child, and I waved her off. "I'm not sick, Ma."

"What's wrong, then?"

"Your husband is crazy."

He scoffed and popped open a lobster tail. He dipped it into the sauce and took a bite.

"What did you do, Joseph Sr.?" Mom glared at him.

"Stop babying that boy. He's over 30 years old."

I laughed at the harsh look on his face. "Somebody's jealous," I teased and tried to reach over the table to grab a piece of catfish. He smacked my hand away. "What are you doing, man?" I argued and tried to do it again.

"I bought this food," Dad said.

"Stop being rude to my baby," Mom said. She lifted the plate and passed it to me.

"That's the problem with him now. He can't find a woman because you're babying him," Dad joked.

My mom flipped him off, and I burst into laughter. "Leave him alone. He is still young and can date around. Just don't bring no babies in this house. I'm too young to be a grandma."

"Woman, you're almost 60." Dad could not help but get at my mom. They did that all the time, and I loved every minute of seeing the playful love in their eyes.

"No, I'm not. I'm still young, and I can have another baby." Mom snapped her fingers and danced in her seat.

The look on my dad's face was priceless, and I wished I had a camera to record the moment. "He needs to grow up, stop flipping between women, and settle down."

"Here we go." I pushed my plate forward, losing my appetite.

"Did you see her in California?" Mom questioned.

I nodded, not ready to have this conversation.

"It was brief," I answered.

"I'm telling you, letting pride get in the way of your happiness will leave your bed cold at night."

I didn't want to drag the conversation out and bring down the good vibe we were having. "What do you want for your anniversary, Ma?"

"Your father is planning on taking me on a cruise." Mom brought her gaze over to me.

"Hmm... Pop, you never want to go anywhere." I leaned back in the seat, arms crossed over my chest, grinning at him.

"Some things, you do for your woman. It's called 'compromise', son," Pop taunted.

My mouth slightly parted, then closed.

"What did you get me?" Mom extended her arm across the table, captured my hand, and stroked the top of it as she smiled.

"It's a surprise."

Her lips formed into a pout. "Fine. Just make sure you come around more for dinner and spend time with your parents."

I chuckled and kissed the side of her cheek, then slapped hands with my dad. "I promise. Let's eat, so I can get home and wash the day away."

We continued talking about the repair shop and the bakery, along with my detailing business. My mom wanted to send me a few items for the community center opening, and I told her to talk with Taylor about what she wanted to bring that day.

An hour later, I got back home and fell into bed without showering. I dozed off, thinking about Jessica's aggravating voice.

Chapter 7

Jessica

I heard the knock from my bedroom, and I dropped my towel, picked up my robe, and went to answer it. I was not expecting any company. I looked out the peephole and saw Scarlett at the door. Unlocking the top lock and chain, I pulled the door open to let her come in.

She was wearing one of her usual high-fashion outfits draped over her thin body. "Bestie!" Scarlett yelled, holding her arms out for an embrace.

"Scarlett, why are you so loud on a weekend afternoon?" I waved her in to take a seat and shut the door. I went back to the bedroom.

She followed. "I missed you, boo." Scarlett sat on my bed.

I stepped into the closet and grabbed a pair of jeans and a t-shirt. I headed to the bathroom to get dressed. "I was only gone for a few days." I put on my jeans and tossed my robe on the back of the bathroom door. I snapped my wireless bra around my back and lifted my shirt above my head.

"A long time in my eyes. I have some juicy news to tell you."

I dipped my head out the bathroom door. "What is it?"

"I fucked Rory again!" She wiggled her brows and giggled.

"Hope you got tested first," I joked, knowing Rory was not the settling-down type, and if she ended up pregnant, then I would help raise the baby.

"Can you be happy for me for once?"

I dropped my eyeliner and stepped out of the bathroom, standing in the doorway and staring at my best friend. People have wondered how we had stayed friends for so long, and I had to tell them that it worked for us, and what we had was genuine. But sometimes, I felt like Scarlett did too much and wanted love in all the wrong places, getting caught up with numerous men who did her no good. "Scarlett, you know I always have your back. Never doubt that."

"But...?"

"You let your insecurities overshadow your judgement of men."

"While you speak about my insecurities, please look in the mirror, boo. You're not too far off."

The guilt washed over me when she stuck that little jab into my heart. I would always have to live with hurting Joseph. Her bringing it up while we were talking about her situation with men was not fair. "You know what? I'm not going there with you, Scarlett. What are we doing today?" I needed some fresh air before I went back to work on my clients' projects. I had not slept one bit since I had been back home from California.

"Sorry, bestie. Let's go to the mall for a little shopping.

My treat." Scarlett got up and walked to my shoe closet. She picked out a pair of heels and held them out for me.

"Thanks. So, tell me about you and Rory." I slid my feet into my black pumps and grabbed my purse and keys off the dresser. I followed her out of my apartment and locked the door.

"He called me while you were out of town, and we had dinner together." Scarlett's hand kept the elevator door from closing. We stepped on and hit the button for the lobby.

"Is he still messing with that girl from the club?" I asked. We'd found out that Rory was a member of Club Escape, along with Joseph, and off and on, he would hook up with some of the women there. I'd told Scarlett not to get serious with him and keep things casual, but she thought it was something more—even though he'd told her from the jump that he was a single man.

I headed to my car and opened the driver's-side door, then slid in, pushing the extra clothes onto the backseat. I had a habit of keeping junk in my car in case of emergencies: clothes, a first-aid kit, a flashlight, and a few gallons of water. I'd hate to get caught stranded somewhere with a dead phone, a dead car battery, and no help coming.

I reversed out of the apartment building and headed toward the light as Scarlett rambled on about Rory. "Probably, but that's fine with me. Once he figures out what he wants, I'll be waiting."

"Scarlett, you can't be serious."

"I'm not sitting at home, waiting on him, Jessica. Unlike you, I know what I want." Her brows lifted in a challenge.

Taking the next right, I stepped on the gas and ignored Scarlett's comment, turning the radio up instead.

"You're ignoring me now?" Scarlett asked.

"No, I'm just thinking."

"About?"

"Joseph."

"He's still keeping a wall up?"

I nodded and turned left at the yellow light, then pulled into the mall entrance and shut the car off. "Something like that. But it's not fair to bring my past mistakes into your situation—even though I think Rory will never change." I picked up my purse and stepped out of the car, then locked up and went to the front entrance.

Scarlett wrapped her arm around my shoulder and pulled me in close. "Friends again?" She held her pinky finger out.

I pushed it away, as we laughed. "Whatever, girl. How is the life of a stylist with Mia Cane going?" Macy's was the first store I pointed to that had a sale sign, so we headed in that direction. I picked up a pair of form-fitting black jeans and lifted them to my waist.

"Good, I'm getting more traveling opportunities—and possibly, my own clients soon."

"That's wonderful. You really should open your own business."

"That's the goal—once I pick up more clientele. I need more high-profile names under my belt." Scarlett sifted through several pieces of clothing on the rack and pulled out a gold dress with black trim on the side. "What do you think of this for Club Escape?"

"It's fine, but a little too short," I said, putting the black jeans back and admiring the shoe section nearby.

"I was thinking of going tomorrow night. You up for coming?" Scarlett asked, following me.

"I can't; I have a lot of work to do."

"Come on, Jessica, you barely go out anymore. One night to take your mind off men problems."

"By going to a sex club?" I asked and put the pair of shoes I'd been admiring back onto the sale rack.

Scarlett waved me off and sucked her teeth. "Not like you're participating in anything. Just watching."

"I'll think about it," I lied, just to end the conversation. I didn't need to go back to that club and run into Joseph again. Who knew what woman he was fucking now?

"Oh! Those would be cute for you." Scarlett snickered, grabbing a pair of tall red bottoms.

"I can barely get around in these kitten heels." I was not into pointy high heels that looked like they could put someone's eye out.

"Just try them on and see, please," she fussed and pushed them into my arms.

I lowered my eyes and squinted at her. My senses were setting off alarms that she was up to something. "What are you up to?" I questioned, sitting on the bench to try the shoes on. I passed her my purse and held my keys out for her to take.

"Nothing. I think you'd look good in them."

"Yeah, right." I stood, angling my feet out and showing off the shoes.

"I think you should get them."

"Maybe, let's keep looking."

"Okay, Mom. But tell me about the party in California."

After placing the shoes back on the rack, we went toward the dress area to see the latest sales. I needed a few more business outfits, and she wanted more dresses for the night life. "Granny enjoyed herself, and I hung out with Angela and Emery."

"How is work going?" Scarlett inquired.

"Everything is good with the business."

"I'm happy for you, babe. Boss Babe Graphics, here we come." Scarlett whistled.

I chuckled as she shimmied in a circle. "I don't see anything I want from here; let's go out to lunch or something," I said. We started to walk out of the store when I felt my phone ringing. "Hello," I answered.

"You remember me? Your father? The other half of your DNA?"

I laughed at my dad's comment. "Hi, Dad. What's going on?"

Scarlett stepped onto the escalator, and I followed.

"I wondered if I could see your face again."

"Daddy, don't start, please."

"You probably stay in contact with your mother more than me," he argued.

I rolled my eyes at his little tantrum. Since they had gotten divorced, I still had to hear them complain about not hearing from me every other week. I was grown now and didn't think that I should have had to check in with them like I was 10. I got to the car and opened the door, tossed my purse to the side, and closed the door. I grabbed the seatbelt with the phone between my shoulder and neck. "Have you talked to your son?" I queried. My brother was a cop. He worked crazy hours, and we barely spent any time together—unless he was coming over to eat up my food.

"I have, and he said he hasn't seen you in a while. So, tell me, what have you been up to?" Dad questioned.

"I'm hanging out with Scarlett right now, Dad. Can I

call you back or stop by tomorrow?" I asked. I felt a pinch on my arm. "Ouch!"

"What's wrong?" Dad asked.

Scarlett waved her hand in the air. "Nothing. Let me call you back."

"Come see me before I end up dropping in on you, little girl," Dad huffed and ended the call without saying goodbye.

I stared at the phone in shock, then placed it in the cup holder, shaking my head at the crazy people in my life.

"Why would you tell him you're coming over tomorrow?" Scarlett leaned against the window and glared at me.

"Um, because he's my dad."

"You promised to go to Club Escape with me tomorrow."

"No, I didn't."

"I'm pretty sure you did."

"When?"

"You promised when you found out that I would be falling all over myself once I saw Rory at the club, and you said that, as a good friend, you couldn't allow that to happen," Scarlett explained.

I ignored her and turned up the music on the radio as she went on and on about what she was going to wear to the club.

30 minutes later, we ended up at the local sub shop around the corner from her place. I parked and strolled in behind her as she talked to someone at the front counter. "Hey, Scarlett," the cashier said.

"Hey, Bree. Can I get the usual, and whatever she wants?" Scarlett pointed back at me.

"I'll get the veggie sub, please, and a water." I started to pull money out of my purse, but she slapped my hand down when I pulled a $20 bill out.

"It's on me."

"This isn't going to convince me to go out with you." I shifted and went to sit in the corner of the shop, near the front entrance. I lifted my phone to check for messages and saw that my brother had texted me.

Micah: Sis, what you cooking?
Me: Nothing.
Micah: This is why you're single now.
Me: Shut up, Micah.
Micah: I'm kidding, sis. You good, though?
Me: Yes, hanging with Scarlett.
Micah: Make sure you have bail money.

I burst into laughter and looked up when Scarlett cleared her throat.

"Who is that?" Scarlett pointed at my phone.

"Micah."

Me: She isn't that bad.
Micah: Shit... not according to Rory.
Me: Are you with him now?

I saw a few dots pop up, and I got nervous, suddenly feeling like he was hanging out with Joseph again. They had their own friendship, separate from me and him, and I never wanted to get in the middle of it, but Micah had told me that if I felt like he should step back from hanging out with them, then he would at the drop of a hat.

Micah: Yeah, is that a problem?

"Here you go, veggie sub and meatball sub with two waters." The cashier dropped our food on the table. We thanked her and dug into the sandwiches.

Me: Nope, enjoy your day.

"Mmmm... this is so good," Scarlett moaned.

"I remember why I stopped coming here. I could eat three of these a day," I said.

Scarlett nodded and took another bite. I unscrewed the cap on the bottled water and took a sip. "What's with Micah?" Scarlett dipped her sandwich into the hot sauce and ate another bite.

"He's hanging with your man," I teased.

She rolled her eyes. "Hush."

We laughed and continued catching up and talking about the latest updates in our lives and families.

Chapter 8

Joseph

I tossed the ball to Rory and placed the money we'd bet on the game in my pocket. It was a 2-on-2 team, with Rory and I against Denver and Micah. On the weekends, some of the kids from school would be out here with us to play, but most had homework, or things to do with their family. I double-tied my shoes and stood, getting in front of Denver, as Micah was on Rory.

"Time out," Rory said, and the game had not even started yet.

"Man, Rory, don't start that bullshit," Denver cursed with his hands on his hips.

"That's what I wanted to tell your sister," Rory taunted.

Denver tried to run after him, and I blocked him. All three of us burst into laughter, but Denver just glared at Rory. His sister and Rory had been on and off for a few years, and they were currently off. Denver hated it because he would always end up getting into fights with them over something stupid after he tried to break up with her—usually because she lied to Denver about what happened.

Micah rebounded the ball and dribbled it up to the point line, then tipped his wrist and launched the ball into the rim. "That's what I'm talking about." Micah said.

I bent down with my hands on my knees, releasing slow breaths. "Easy one for you," I joked, clapped my hands.

"Bro, you didn't let me have that," Micah fussed back.

"Here, your turn," Rory said, pushing the ball toward Denver and crossing it in front of him. Rory went for the defense and slapped the ball out of his hand.

"You talk to my sister?" Micah asked.

I dipped my brows low, wondering why this was being brought up now. "Why?"

"I just talked to her, and she's hanging with Scarlett," Micah said.

"Aw, shit." Rory shook his head and walked near the benches.

"What's up with you and Scarlett?" Denver questioned, following him.

"Man, she's crazy. I thought I'd been with crazy women before, but Scarlett takes the cake," Rory complained. Micah and I stood on the court, doing one-off shots back and forth.

"That's what happens when you take things outside the club and into your house," Denver remarked. I glanced over at him, thinking about my first time with Jessica in my office, when I heard her seductive moans and cries of pleasure in my ear. "Take Joseph over here!" Denver called out.

"Keep me out of your theories, homeboy," I mugged his ass.

"He's in his feelings now," Rory joked.

I squared and shadow-boxed with him. "Fuck you, Rory—and you, too, Denver." I chuckled and waved him off.

"Man, y'all fools need a comedy show or something. I'm ready to go eat," Denver said.

"I could eat," Micah agreed.

"We can hit up a bar and have some drinks," Rory suggested. I nodded and checked my watch. It was late, and I had nothing really planned for the night beyond working on business investment proposals.

"Well, nobody won, so we're even today," Denver said.

"Don't Rory still owe you for last week?" Micah asked, grabbing his bag and heading to his truck.

All of us burst into laughter at the harsh grimace on Denver's face at Rory, giggling like a schoolgirl. "Double it for next week to make it interesting," I suggested, then hopped in my car and shut the door. Rory got in on the passenger side and tossed his gym bag in the back.

Denver went with Micah, who was parked in front of us. "Let's meet at 42 Bar in an hour!" Micah yelled. I nodded, rolling the window down farther and turning the bass on the stereo up. I made a U-turn in the middle of the street from the side of the courtyard.

"Drop me off, and I'll meet you there," Rory said, typing away on his phone.

I chuckled, knowing it was some booty call he was answering and would be showing up later than the rest of us. "Better strap up or get ready for the Maury Show to call," I joked, hitting the gas and heading down the street to his place in Queens.

"So, what's up with you and Scarlett's homegirl?"

Rory glanced in my direction.

I shifted gears and stepped on the gas, heading onto the highway. "Nothing. Why are you asking me about her?" My nostrils flared at the mention of her from his mouth.

"Dude, for somebody that says they're over their ex, you're sure looking at me hard, like you want to punch me in the face." Rory slid his phone into his pocket.

I focused on the traffic again. "Rory, you're the last person who needs to bring up exes—*or* current relationships."

He furrowed his brows. "What? Like I am offended that you think so little of me, bro?" Rory cackled.

I punched him in the arm. "Man, shut up." I pulled up to his place 20 minutes later, and he got out and headed into his building. I honked the horn to let him know that I was driving off.

* * *

42 Bar was blasting old-school rap and R&B music. Rory and I pushed through the crowd and sat at the bar next to Micah. It was just the three of us because Denver had an emergency with his baby-mama. She was calling back-to-back about him picking up his son from the hospital because he'd had an allergic reaction.

I waved for the bartender to order another round of shots. The bartender winked, slid three glasses across the bar, and poured each of us a round. I slid her a $100 bill as a tip. She was pretty, with a short bob, full lips, and tattoos running down both her arms. She was wearing a short skirt that showed off her plump ass. But the way she flirted with the women at the bar showed she was not playing for my team.

I felt a hand on my shoulder and looked over at Rory, who was grinning. "Man, it's sexy women here tonight."

"Yeah, too many to choose from," Micah hinted at the two women staring back at us by the end of the bar.

"I might have to take somebody home tonight," Rory mentioned.

I turned toward him as he pulled over a woman who walked by him and whispered in her ear. She slapped him across the face, and I chuckled at his smirk. "Fool, you keep thinking these women want that toxic love that you're throwing at them," I said.

He shrugged and rubbed the sting away. "She wants me," Rory said.

"That's *your* friend," Micah told me.

"I don't claim him," I replied.

"Micah, tell this fool he needs to get his act together and talk to your sister," Rory said, leaning over the bar and picking up the third shot glass.

"They're both grown. I told Jessica the same thing," Micah said.

"We can coexist without drama, Rory," I replied.

"Ooh, what's up, ladies? How are you doing?" Rory said to the last person I thought would be there, standing in front of me.

Natasha licked her lips as she stared at me. I scratched the back of my neck, nervous about what was going to come out of her mouth. She stepped between my legs and placed her hands on my thighs. "I didn't expect to see you here tonight?" Natasha said.

I gently removed her hands and pushed her back, giving us space. "What's up?"

Rory and Micah burst out laughing.

Natasha did not like to be turned down, but she was stepping into my personal space when I'd already told her that I was not interested in anything beyond what we'd done in the past. "Really, Joseph?" Natasha spat.

"Listen, if my boy doesn't want to take you for a ride, you can always look at me, baby," Rory commented. Micah shook his head at him.

"Rory, get the fuck out of here!" Natasha shouted, pushing him away.

He held his hands up in surrender and cackled like a 15-year-old.

"Natasha, we've talked about this already, and my mind hasn't changed," I said.

"Fine. But don't think you'll forget about all this." Natasha gripped her ass, then swished off with her friends next to her.

"Damn!" Rory shouted.

I ran a hand down my face in frustration. Even when I was trying to focus on myself and my career, women were still driving me crazy.

* * *

An hour later, after hanging with Micah and Rory, I had drunk five shots and two beers, but I was not too wasted after I got some water in me. Once I'd left the bar, I was driving around thinking, and I found myself in front of Jessica's apartment. I knew she was still up because she often worked late at my place when were together. I knocked on the door of the house I'd come to, hoping to get what I needed without an argument.

"What are you doing here so late?" She was wearing glasses, a big t-shirt, and slippers, with her bare thighs out and her freckles perfectly etched across her face. Her hair was up in a scarf.

I found myself smiling at her—even though I shouldn't have given in to her pretty, poked-out bottom lip, and her hands on her hips. "I wanted to get my bag."

"Now?!" she growled, throwing her hands in the air. Her face scrunched up.

I swear, my heart fluttered at her getting all riled up. "I thought it wouldn't be a problem since you work late sometimes."

"That's beside the point, Joseph. You should have called first," she sassed, then turned to let me walk inside. I closed the door, peeking around at her apartment. She walked into the other room to grab my luggage. I plopped down on the couch, leaned my head back, and closed my eyes briefly. I felt my chest tighten at the bag being dropped into my lap. "Here," Jessica said, then walked in front of me and took a seat on the other end of the couch.

I licked my lips at the way her shirt rode up her thighs. She drew her legs underneath her and pulled some papers into her lap. "What are you doing?" I questioned, snatching them out of her hands.

"Hey!" she shouted and tried to get them back. She leaned over my lap, and I held the papers high with one hand, then put the other hand on her waist. "Give me those." Jessica lifted herself off the couch, and her breast ended up in my face. I gently bit her nipple. "Joseph!" she whined, scooting back.

I had a tight grip around her waist. "What, Freckles?" I teased, squeezing her waist.

"Can I please have my work back?" she asked nicely. I grinned and shook my head. "You're still an asshole, I see."

"Takes one to know one." I looked at what she was working on. It had me and Brent's real estate logo on it. "This looks dope," I said.

"You think so?"

I shifted her in my lap, and we looked at them together. "Yeah, you have great skills."

"Thanks." She stared at me.

I felt my hard-on poke her in the ass, and she tried to wiggle out of my hold. "Why are you trying to move?" I questioned.

"Because this isn't right."

"Says who?" I asked, dropping the papers on the floor. I grasped the back of her neck and peered into her eyes, then leaned my head up to capture her mouth.

At first, she tensed, then loosened up, wrapping both her hands around my neck and pulling me in close. "Mmm..." she moaned.

My hand slid up and down her back. I squeezed my eyes tight, remembering all our nightly lovemaking and hearing her screams of passion. "What did you do to me, Jessica?" I bit her bottom lip, ran a hand across her cheek, and then pulled back, staring at her swollen lips.

"Joseph..." she whimpered.

My hand went down her back and under her shirt, then into her panties, feeling how wet she was just from one kiss. "She misses me," I said, kissing her cheek, under her ear, and down her shoulder.

"Yes," she said.

"Do *you* miss me?" I stopped moving my finger in and out of her wet folds and stared into her eyes. I did not want this to be about sex. I needed to know that I was not the only one who felt the same agony of emptiness.

"Always. I was stupid, J."

"What else?" I continued trailing kisses over her skin and started to lift her shirt over her head.

"I apologize. I was stupid, like I said. I let my old feelings destroy what we were building," Jessica said.

I nodded, feeling the sincerity in her voice. "I apologize for cutting you out of my life and not hearing you out fully. Did you sleep with him?" A part of me hoped that they had not gone that far, but I knew that with rekindled romances, couples would jump each other's bones in a second.

She shook her head. "No, it was a few dates and talking, but honestly, I was always thinking about you when I was with him," Jessica remarked.

I was taken aback by her statement. "So, what are we going to do, then?"

"About what?" she asked, fiddling with her hands.

"About this." I pointed between the both of us.

"I..." she started to say, but her phone rang. I groaned and removed my hands. I saw the name Eric flash across the screen. I glared at her, then moved her off my lap and stood. "Joseph, wait! It's not what you think," she said, following me.

I reached down and grabbed my bag, then strolled to the door. "Save it, Jessica."

"He's been calling nonstop for weeks, and I've been ignoring him," she said.

I waved her off and opened the door, then turned and looked over my shoulder. "Until you can get that handled, we won't work." I walked out as she continued calling my name. I headed out of her building and back to my car to go home and drink away my erection, and the nasty thoughts I was having about fucking her with her legs behind her head, like I used to do.

Chapter 9

Jessica

A week later, Joseph still was not taking my calls —unless it was about business—and I had to admit to myself that I understood the reason. We had been like a roller coaster ride of emotions, dealing with people that did not mean us any good. Right now, I was at the coffee shop, waiting for Eric to show up, so I could end the little games he was playing. I had not been sexually active with anyone in over seven months, and the last time, it was with Joseph. So, having him in my space and remembering all the things we'd done together had made me need a release bad. After Joseph left, I turned my phone off and grabbed my little bullet vibrator that Angela had recommended to me. I took matters into my own hands and pictured Joseph bringing me to the edge of ecstasy with his lips, hands, and dick.

"Hey, babe," Eric said, startling me out of my thoughts. He tried to kiss me on the lips. I pushed him away. He took a seat across from me. "What's wrong?"

"*You're* what's wrong," I hissed.

His brows dipped in confusion. He tried to reach over

the table and grab my hand. "What's the problem, Jessica?"

"My problem is you, thinking we're some couple, when we're not. I don't want you."

His head lowered in shame. I did not feel bad. I thought my world was over when he broke up with me, and I had to start all over again. Was Eric handsome? Yes, but it was not all about being cut and having money. I wanted someone who wanted me in all ways and appreciated me. That was Joseph, and I'd let my foolish mind get clouded and let Eric talk me back into trying a relationship again. I was dumb and gullible, but the Jessica who let him walk all over me the first time was no more.

"Baby."

"No, all I want is for you to leave me alone and go back to the tramp you started cheating on me with in the first place. I'm done with you, Eric."

"Is it someone else?"

"Yes," I said and waited for him to respond.

His eyes narrowed into slits, and his fists clenched on the table. I was not scared of him, and he had never hit me, but the reaction I was getting was exactly how I'd felt when he dumped me for another girl and said I was bad in bed. "You'll be back," Eric insisted, standing and leaning across the table.

"I finally found what I was looking for."

"He'll leave you, like I did. You're not worth it, Jess."

"It's Jessica, asshole," I spat. I watched him stomp out of the shop, and relief washed over me after finally confronting him about all the past hurt. I took a sip of my chai latte as I scrolled through my phone. The only thing on my agenda was finishing up the design for Joseph and sneaking over to his office since he had avoided all contact with me after he left my place last week. Angela's name popped onto my screen, and I answered, taking another sip, "Hello."

"Tell me why I shouldn't divorce my husband," Angela said.

I giggled, knowing how dramatic Angela could get if she did not have her way. Brent spoiled her and the kids, but she needed control of everything, and he was just the guy to put her in her place when she needed to calm down. "What's the problem?" I asked, as the barista brought my usual chocolate muffin to me at my table.

"I wanted to go shopping for the baby's nursery, and he's talking about how I need to sit my butt down," Angela snapped.

I heard fussing in the background. It sounded like a man and a woman. "Where are you?"

"At Granny's with the kids and Brent."

"Family dinner?" I inquired.

She sucked her lips and whispered through the phone, "Save me."

I burst into laughter as the phone sounded like it had dropped in a scuffle. "Angela! Angela!"

"Sit down, little girl. Hello, Jessica?" Granny Lynn said.

"Yes, ma'am?"

"Don't listen to Angela's bigheaded behind. Brent offered to let her do online shopping with his card because the doctor said she needs to stay off her feet," Granny informed me.

I nodded, pulling a piece of my muffin top off and tossing it into my mouth. "I know she's being stubborn."

"Stubborn is the least of our problems. She's so damn spoiled," Granny mentioned.

I chortled. Granny was just as spoiled by the entire family, so she could see herself in Angela. All the husbands pampered Granny with whatever she needed, along with Pops. It was just a matter of time before they made them retire for good and stop watching the kids so much.

"Old woman, give me my phone back," I heard through the phone.

"Angela, you might scare your husband, but not me, sweetie. Don't take a leap when you climb this tree, honey," Granny replied.

I could hear everyone in the background, laughing at the mess that had come out of her mouth. "Oh, my God! You two are ridiculous. I have business that I need to take care of."

"What business?" Granny asked.

I removed some money from my purse for a tip and bagged up my muffin, then strolled outside to my car. "Presenting the final logo to Joseph."

"Oh, that handsome fella is still sniffing around?" Granny asked.

I dropped into the driver's seat and reached back for my seatbelt. "We've talked and made amends," I lied. It was only semi-better between us, but she did not need to know that.

"Lie to somebody who doesn't know you, Jessica," Granny said.

I heard the phone drop. "Girl, don't listen to her," Angela said, coming back on the line.

"I won't if you start to listen to your husband."

"He's being mean," Angela simpered.

I blew out a breath, just trying to imagine how Brent put up with her. I wondered if Joseph felt the same way about me. "Well, Angela, we both know you can be just as vicious."

A loud gasp caused me to remove the phone from my ear. "I thought it was blood before anything else, Jessica?" Angela asked.

"I'll always have your back, but you need to listen to him—*and* the doctor."

"Fine. What's up with you?" Angela asked.

"Nothing much. Heading to meet with Joseph now."

"Are things better with you two? I'm ready to throw another bachelorette party. You're the last single girl in the group," Angela mentioned.

"Slow your roll. Marriage is nowhere near my line of sight." I drove off into traffic, switching to Bluetooth.

"It could be if you talked to the man and put that loving on him."

"We almost went there last time, but he stopped it."

"Oh, tell me everything."

"Nope. You have to suffer and think about why you're being hard on your husband."

"I thought you loved me," Angela sniffed.

I rolled my eyes. All the hormones of a pregnant woman had taken place throughout this call. "Are you crying?"

"Bitch, no," Angela spat.

I slapped the steering wheel, laughing as her attitude changed that fast. "Please stay off your feet and let your man pamper you."

"Whatever. How is Scarlett doing?"

"She's good, still running after Rory," I sighed, thinking of how my friend had gone from being a jet-setting free spirit to being boy crazy all because of Rory's dog ass.

"Well, at least you got the good guy out of the equation," Angela said.

"Scarlett would say different." A few minutes later, I finally made it to his office building, and I parked near the exit, so as not to block the incoming and outgoing cars. I grabbed my portfolio and switched Bluetooth off to end the call with Angela. "Angela, I made it to my appointment. Let me call you back."

"Okay, don't forget to call me when you get a chance. I need all the gossip, now that I'm homebound," Angela said.

I agreed and ended the call as I stepped into the reception area of his office.

"Jessica! Don't you look cute today?" Patty announced.

I had not been the best at keeping up with everyone at the shop since I left, but Patty had always been the sweetest. "Thanks, Patty. How are you doing?" I took a seat in the chair in the lobby and crossed my legs. I was prepared to wait for Joseph to talk to me—even if it took all day.

"I'm doing good, girl. My children are well and happy. How is the business going?"

"Right now, I have three clients, and I'm slowly growing. I'm excited."

"Well, I know you'll do fantastic. Does Joseph know you're here?" she asked and lifted the phone to make him aware.

I held my hand out to stop her. "It's a surprise, actually."

She looked nervous, gnawing on her upper lip and not making eye contact. "Um, Jessica, he's in the middle of a meeting."

"That's fine. I don't mind waiting."

His office door opened, and a bubbly laugh wafted through the room, along with Joseph's. I watched him walk out with a woman, side by side, and his hand was on her lower back. *Do I have a right to be jealous?* I thought.

"Jessica!" Joseph called out.

In my jumbled state, I looked between them. I cleared my throat and stood, then reached my hand out to shake. "Hi, I'm Jessica. His girlfriend," I said boldly, with a smile on my face.

She gasped in shock and looked over at Joseph.

"Jessica, go to my office," he said.

"Joseph, what is she talking about?" the woman asked. She was shorter than me, with way more curves, and bigger up top.

"Nothing. I'll talk to you later, Taylor," Joseph said and escorted her out. I marched into his office and dropped my portfolio on his desk, then crossed my arms and tapped my foot as I waited for him to return. I heard arguing in the front, with Joseph telling Patty that she should have told me to call first. Five minutes later, he came into his office and slammed the door, then took a seat at his desk. "What can I do for you, Jessica?"

"You can start by telling me who that woman was to you." I pointed to the door with my nostrils flared, and my eyes throwing daggers at his face.

"I don't owe you an explanation."

"Stop playing games with me, Joseph. I have tried to call you for the past week to get together, so I can apologize. We had a meeting scheduled the next day, and you canceled." I stomped my feet and walked around to his desk, then pointed in his face.

"And?"

"I love you!" I shouted, feeling weak, with tears

pooling in my eyes. This man ignited my soul and could also break me in every way possible. Giving that much control to someone was not what I wanted when I slept with them for the first time, but love did not give me a handbook.

"Come here." He reached a hand out for me to take, and I let him pull me into his lap, with my legs straddling him. He lifted my chin and wiped my tears from my cheeks. "She doesn't mean anything to me. Taylor's planning the center opening."

"Really? The way she got upset when I said 'girlfriend' seemed like it was more."

"She asked me out, but I always turn her down."

"Why?"

"You know why." His hand slid up my bare leg, then up my thigh. He gripped the back of my neck and forced our noses to touch as we sucked in each other's air.

"Tell me," I whispered, running a hand up his chest and gripping his jacket.

"I love you and only you. Every time I think I'm ready to move on, I see your face in my mind." Joseph ran his tongue across my bottom lip, opening my mouth and sucking on my tongue.

I groaned and grinded on his lap. "Did you lock the door?" I asked, not wanting Patty to walk in on us.

"She knows to hold all calls and not let anybody in here," Joseph answered, and I felt better about what could happen in here. I could still remember the first time he had me on top of his desk and fucked me so good that I could still feel him hours later. "Take this off," he demanded and removed my jacket, then lifted my dress over my head.

I was in only my panties, bra, and heels. He sucked on

my neck, and I grasped the back of his head. He buried his face against my neck. "Oh... Joseph."

"You looked sexy as fuck, bossing me around like that. I liked that shit, and my dick got so hard," Joseph confessed.

I smirked. "Good, that's your first warning. Cut off all your playthings because I am back and never leaving again." He lifted me with my legs wrapped around his waist and planted me on top of the desk. "Wait!" I said, halting his efforts to unbuckle his pants.

"What now, Freckles?"

"I came to show you the designs."

"Can't we do that later? My mind is kind of on something else," Joseph said.

I rolled my eyes. "On one condition."

"You're not really in the position to negotiate since you were in the wrong."

"Don't make me call Patty in here."

He groaned and slapped me on my thigh, then bent down to kiss my lips. "What's the condition?"

"You agree to the logo—no matter what it looks like."

"What do I get out of this?" Joseph asked, rubbing circles on my thigh and hip as he grinded his pelvis against me.

"A very sloppy, nasty blowjob, plus dinner on me later." I held my hand out for a shake.

He looked at me skeptically but slid his palm into mine. "Fine, I agree. Now, can I enjoy this alone time with my woman officially?" Joseph questioned.

I dropped the papers on the floor and unsnapped my bra. "Enjoy, baby."

He grunted and grasped both my breasts in his hands, flicking his tongue across each. I gripped the back of his neck and squirmed in his arms as he sucked like a newborn baby. "Joseph... baby." I'd felt my pussy throbbing from the first second he put his hands on me, but now I was leaking through my panties and down my thighs. This man was like a puppet master, and I had no control over my body as he worked me over so well.

"Shit, you feel so good in my arms." He ripped my panties off and dropped to his knees, then swiped his tongue across my bare lower lips.

I clutched both my breasts as he worked me to the highest level of orgasm. He stroked and tweaked, while one hand covered one of mine on my breast, then he inserted a finger into my pussy, and I almost arched off the desk. "Joseph! Ahhh, wait, baby." I tried to cover my mouth. Hopefully, no one heard me.

He slapped it down. "Stop that. I don't care if they hear us; this is my business, and you're my woman."

"I... I... can't. Oh, God, Joseph."

He stuck a second finger inside, twisting and scissoring quickly. "Come for me, baby!" Joseph called out, and like clockwork, I convulsed and shook in his arms. He stood up and kissed me on the lips sensually, then ran a hand across my stomach.

My eyes tried to stay open and watch as he pulled my favorite thing out of his boxers. His thick, heavy, long third leg was looking especially delicious as precum glistened at the tip. I reached down and stroked him a few times, then wiped off his seed and stuck it in my mouth.

"Remember, I love you, Jessica. The minute I put him inside you, it's over. You're my woman, and that's it for everybody from the past," Joseph announced.

I nodded, taking the condom out of his hand and rolling it over his erection. "Fuck me." I opened my legs wider, reaching down to show him what awaited him. My core was so wet; it was dripping down my ass. I stuck my finger into his mouth, so he could taste it again.

"Perfect." he said, sliding inside slowly, and then stopping.

"Ugh. You feel so good," I muttered, running a hand up his muscular chest. He hovered over my body and kissed me, sticking his tongue inside my mouth. Then he stood, staring at me lustily.

Chapter 10

Joseph

I bit my lip, thinking about how much time had passed between us since I last held her in my arms. I did not want to rush making up with her and exploring every enticing curve of her body. Looking down into her eyes, I thought of all the dirty things I wanted to do to her body to make up for lost time. I had not gone to Club Escape since I saw her there the first time with Scarlett. Now, she was underneath me, with her warm walls choking my erection. I could stay there in that moment forever.

"I can barely breathe; I feel you in my stomach." She moved her head from side to side.

I eased out, leaving just the tip. I did that a few times to get her used to me again. "Am I the only one that's been in you since last year?" I asked, slammed into her core as my nails dug into her hips. I got a good rhythm going as the desk started to move. She nodded, but I wanted to hear her words. "Talk to me, baby; let me hear you. Fuck being quiet."

"Yes... only you."

"Fuck!" I watched as my dick glistened from her juices, then licked my lips, thinking of her sweet taste on my tongue.

"Ahh!" she screamed, gripping the top of the desk and trying to hold on.

I pounded into her cave, making up for lost time. She only got wetter and wetter as my dick found its way back home, and my spine stiffened; my orgasm was nearing. "Ahh... shit! Come for me, baby."

"I love you!" Jessica moaned as she came on my desk and my dick.

I was right behind her, and I collapsed on top of her, out of breath. She rubbed my back as I slowly eased out of her and sat back in the chair. I pulled her into my lap. "Where are you headed after this?" I questioned, searing her lips with a kiss and pushing a finger into her swollen pussy. I watched her eyes flutter and fight to stay open.

"Home. I was supposed to meet Scarlett for dinner," she muttered.

"Come home with me."

"Okay."

We kissed again, and I let her get up to get dressed. She picked up her purse and pulled some wipes out, then passed me one. I cleaned up and tossed it in the trash, then zipped my pants and fixed the desk.

"Do you have any meetings lined up for today?" Jessica questioned, sliding her dress down.

I watched her fat pussy glisten. "I told Patty I'm taking the rest of the day off."

"I'm starving. You want to stop and grab something to eat?"

"We'll order on the way home and pick it up."

I escorted her out of my office. Denver and Willy

were walking inside with bags of food in their hands. "What's up, Jessica?" Denver asked, leaning down to give her a hug.

"Hi, Denver. Willy, you staying out of trouble?" Jessica teased.

He smirked and stepped closer into her space, and I held my hand out and nudged him back. "Off-limits, playboy."

"Wait, you two official now? Like a couple?" Willy asked.

Jessica giggled and locked her arm with mine. I slid an arm around her waist and drew her against my side. "None of your business."

Jessica slapped me on the chest. I furrowed my brows. "Stop being rude, baby," Jessica said.

"Yeah, Joseph, listen to your lady. Not nice, being rude." Willy rubbed his hands together, and I popped him on the back of his head. "Ouch! Man. See, Jessica? He needs to be on punishment," Willy argued.

I pushed him out of the way and took Jessica by the hand. We walked out of the office and down to my car. I opened the passenger side and let her sit, then shut the door. I jogged around to the driver's side and grabbed my seatbelt.

"Wait!" she said. "My car is here."

"It'll be fine; I'll text Denver to drop it off at my place later."

"Are you sure? I don't want to put anyone out."

"He'll be fine."

She pulled her keys out of her purse, and I grabbed them. I ran back inside to give them to Patty, then stepped back out of the office and into the car. I started the ignition, backed out of my space, and turned to head toward the light. I stopped at the stop sign and leaned over to kiss her on the lips. I grasped her hand in mine as I drove home.

Once we picked up our food after ordering through the app, I let her step off the elevator and walk ahead of me with the key to my apartment as I carried the bags. I slapped her on the ass, watching it jiggle, then rubbed the sting away as I pushed up on her with my dick, poking her in the ass while she tried to concentrate on opening the door. I reached around and rubbed her stomach, then up towards her breasts, engulfing both in one hand while I grinded against her slowly.

"Baby... stop." She giggled. I tried to reach down and slide my hand underneath her dress, but she pushed me back with her butt. "Nope, we need to eat first."

We walked in and shut the door behind us. She followed me to the kitchen, and I placed the food on the counter and grabbed some plates and utensils, so we could eat the dumplings, shrimp vermicelli with steamed garlic, and egg rolls. "What do you want to drink?" I asked.

"What do you have?" She took her jacket off and removed the food from the bags, then started to plate everything.

"I got water, soda, wine, and hard liquor if you're in the mood." I wiggled my brows.

"Wine is fine." Jessica picked up our plates, walked to the living room, and set them on the table. She kicked off her shoes. I popped the bottle of white wine and poured us a glass, then went to sit by her on the floor. "I could get used to this," she said, putting her legs over my lap as we started to eat.

"I hope so."

"So, tell me what women you have been with since we were apart."

I choked on the first bite of dumpling from her question, and she patted me on the back. "What kind of question is that?"

"Tell me. I won't be mad. I just need to know what I'm up against." Jessica pushed her food around on her plate.

"Baby, you're not up against anything. I told you, it is me and you only. Did I have a few people I talked with? Yes, but nothing serious."

"I bought a vibrator and named him Joseph," she blurted out, hiding her face in my chest.

I laughed and put both our plates on the table. I maneuvered her to straddle my lap and removed her dress. "You know what attracted me to you?" I asked.

"What?"

"Your personality. Don't get me wrong; you're a beautiful woman, but baby, you're goofy as fuck."

She smacked me on the chest and crossed her arms, causing her breasts to lift. My eyes darkened at her chocolate-drop areolas showing through her shirt. I knew she was still swollen from our earlier sex session, but I planned on making up for lost time before the night was over. "Fuck you, Joseph."

"I'd love for that to happen, but your pussy is screaming to get a break." Her mouth dropped wide open and she tried to jump up, but I held her down by the waist and took her breasts in my mouth. "Stop pouting." I released them after tweaking each nipple.

"I might prefer my vibrator over you. At least he stays quiet," she joked, mushing me in the head.

"Tell me how your parents are doing. I talk to your brother all the time, but not them."

"They're good. Constantly trying to drive me crazy but fine. Micah told me you had a ball the other week."

"Yeah, we try to get together on the weekends to catch up."

"How are your parents?" she asked.

"Good. About to have an anniversary, and I'm throwing a surprise party."

"That's cool. Micah told me about the center. What's going on with that?"

"Taylor, the girl you met earlier, she's doing the event decorations and setting everything up. I have a few sponsors, and things are running smooth."

"Taylor seems to love her job."

"She does, and I don't need you getting crazy. She knows I'm taken."

"Does she?"

"Yes." I pecked her lips and tapped her to get up. I grabbed her hand, walked her to the bedroom, and grabbed a shirt for her to change into. I wasn't going out for the rest of night, and neither was she. It was time to reconnect and catch up. "Jump in the shower, and I'll meet you in bed in a few minutes."

"Where are you going?" she questioned.

"I'll take the guest bathroom. Otherwise, we'll never get clean if I follow you." I pressed a kiss to her forehead and grabbed my pajamas, then walked out of my room toward the second bathroom upstairs. 30 minutes later, I walked into the bedroom and saw that she was knocked out in my bed on the side that I liked to sleep on. I shook my head. I lifted the covers and climbed in, scooting her over gently and wrapping a hand around her waist. I turned the game on low as she slept.

"I'm not asleep," Jessica mumbled.

"Could have fooled me." I put the remote down and curled up behind her with my chest to her back. I reached around to the front of her shirt and slid a finger into her core. She opened for me, gasping from the intrusion. I kissed her on the side of her neck, moving my finger in and out slowly. "Throw that damn vibrator away. The only thing that should be touching you is me."

"Ahh... oh."

"You hear me, Freckles?" I slid a second finger into her folds.

"Yes..."

I pushed my pajamas down and popped my dick out, then lifted her leg and eased my dick inside slowly. Her pussy was already choking on my dick. "Yeah, you need to toss that damn toy out." I started to get annoyed, just thinking of her using a damn toy. My thrusts started to get faster, and the sounds of our bodies slapping together filled the room. I rolled her onto her stomach and pushed her hands above her head, then whispered in her ear as I kept a steady rhythm, "Fuck, baby, your pussy feels so good."

"Mmm... shit." She buried her head in the pillow to muffle her cries.

"Naw, I need to hear your words, baby. Tell me how your feel." I licked from the bottom of her spine to her neck.

She shivered and tried to move in my arms. I held her legs straight, driving into her deep. "I love you... oh, fuck... I'm coming." She trembled in my arms. I pulled out, releasing my seed onto her back, then fell to the side of her to catch my breath. "I guess I can get rid of my vibrator now," she kidded.

I smacked her on the ass and hopped up to grab a wet towel out of the bathroom and clean her up. I dropped it on the night table and pulled her against my chest. We fell asleep together while the TV played. It was the best sleep I'd had in a long time.

* * *

A month later, we had been going back and forth, staying at each other's place and fucking like rabbits while she continued to work from home. I offered to help her get an office to work in, but she did not want any handouts, and I could respect that.

Today, we were heading to my parents' house for a visit. My mom called and wanted to have dinner in the backyard with our family and friends. I told her I was not up for a big crowd, but Jessica said that if I wanted to get another sloppy blowjob, then I had to go. So, here I was, parking in front of my parents' house, ready to get this shit over with, so we could head back home.

I picked up Jessica's hand and kissed the back of it, then pressed a kiss on her lips. I opened the door to come around and help her out of the passenger side.

"What do you think your parents will think of me?" she asked.

I shrugged, not knowing or really caring because it wouldn't change how I felt about her. "What they think doesn't matter. Yes, I would like for them to love you as much as I do, but it won't stop me from loving you."

"I just feel bad because they know me as the girl who broke their son's heart."

"They'll get over it. Besides, you've made up for a lot of lost time." I groped her plump ass.

"My vagina is going on lockdown, sir."

I jerked my head back and scoffed.

"Oh, my God, look at your face right now, Joseph. Calm down; I was just joking."

"Baby, I play about a lot of things. Pussy ain't one of them," I said, grasping her hand and heading to my parents' front door.

"I've been meaning to ask you—have you gone back to Club Escape?" she asked.

The door flew open before I could knock, and Rory was standing there, with a smirk on his face. "Well, if it isn't the lovebirds," Rory said.

"What are you doing here?" I questioned and pushed him aside to walk in. I noticed Scarlett, talking in the corner to some woman.

"I was invited by Micah," Rory said and sipped on his beer.

"Who did you come with?"

"Scarlett. What's up, Jessica?" Rory gave her a hug.

She released my hand to go toward Scarlett, and I pulled her back to stay close. "Baby, I'm just going to talk to Scarlett," Jessica said.

"I'll come with you," I said.

"Don't be silly; I can handle walking into a room by myself," Jessica replied and took off toward her friend.

Rory grinned devilishly. "Yeah, you should probably have this right now. You need it more than me." He passed me his beer. I pushed it away and almost felt like I needed to vomit when Jessica pointed over at me, and Natasha glanced our way. "You sure you don't want a drink?" Rory asked.

I glared at him. "What the fuck is she doing here?" I marched over to her and cut into the conversation.

"Hey, baby, this is Natasha," Jessica said.

Natasha reached her hand out for a shake. "We've already met. How are you, Joseph?" Natasha asked. My stomach dropped and twisted in knots.

Jessica looked between us, and I felt sweat bead on my forehead. "How do you two know each other?" Jessica questioned.

"My baby boy!" Mom came into the living room and hugged me around the waist. "You made it in time. I have all your favorites."

I was barely paying her any attention as I glowered at Natasha. She was pissing me off, constantly showing up in places that I frequented, and now at my parents' house. "Who invited you here?" I asked.

"I did," Scarlett said.

"Wait, how do you know her?" Jessica asked.

"She goes to Club Escape, and we've hung out a few times." Scarlett responded.

"Hello, who are you?" My mom extended her hand toward Natasha. I gripped Natasha's arm and walked her off toward the front door.

"What the fuck?!" Scarlett shouted, marching behind me and yelling at Rory to stop me.

"Let me go, Joseph," Natasha said. I opened the door and started to walk her to the sidewalk.

A crowd started to form at the front door. "Joseph, what in the hell is going on?" Mom started to walk down the steps.

I held my hand up. "Go back in the house!"

"Joseph!" Jessica did not listen and stomped toward us.

I poked my finger in Natasha's face. "Get the fuck out of here now, or I'll have Micah arrest you for stalking," I barked. I stopped Jessica before she could get any closer. I turned her back around toward the house.

"Joseph, you know she can't please you like I can," Natasha taunted.

Whispers and murmurs flooded the porch. Jessica twisted out of my hold and pushed me back to get in Natasha's face. "I don't know who you are, and I don't really care, but this one right here belongs to me. What you had with him at the club is over. Done. Finished."

Natasha waved Jessica off and curled her lip at her. "He's done nothing but call and ask me to come back, wanting to make us a real thing, so are you sure about that, sweetie?" Natasha lied, knowing damn well I hadn't spoken to her since the bar. I hoped Jessica wouldn't fall for her bullshit.

"Do I look like I believe you, Nikki, Natalie, whatever your name is?"

"It's Natasha."

"Good for you. He told you to leave, and I suggest you do it before you can't keep your teeth in your mouth." Jessica poked Natasha in the shoulder. I grabbed her by the arm to pull her back, and Natasha took that as her chance to mush her in the head. "Bitch!" Jessica yelled and tried to get around me to fight Natasha, who walked off to her car.

I wrapped my arms around Jessica and whispered in her ear, "Baby, let it go." I rubbed up and down her arms.

"Let me go, Joseph," she said calmly.

"No."

"Joseph... let me go."

"Not until you calm down and don't try to leave."

She released a harsh breath. "Mrs. Michaels, will you please tell your son to let me go?"

"Joseph, I told you to not be out here, playing around with crazy women. Let her go and come inside."

"She'll try to leave, though."

"No, she won't." Mom peered at Jessica, and she dropped her head in confirmation.

I finally released her, and she headed back inside. I felt a tightness in my chest, worried this would only lead us back to Square One. Finally, the show was over, and I got back inside and looked around for Jessica. "Where did she go?" I asked Rory.

"She's talking with Scarlett and your mom."

"Damn."

"Yeah, you fucked up me getting laid tonight, man," Rory joked.

"Rory, shut the fuck up," I spat and glared at him.

"Listen, I know you're pissed, but she didn't know about y'all."

I rubbed my temples and sat on the couch. He passed me a beer. "You're right. My bad."

"Besides, Jessica didn't leave, and she's talking with your mom. So, you still got her in the bag."

"Do you ever take anything seriously?" I wondered, taking another gulp of beer.

"Um, getting pussy," Rory replied.

I pushed him away from me and jumped up to search for Jessica.

Chapter 11

Jessica

Scarlett was trying to convince me to leave with her, and his Mom was telling me to stay and cool off. My head was spinning in two different directions, and I was worried that I was making a big mistake by committing to Joseph, knowing his sexual appetite was high.

"I'm sorry, Mrs. Michaels, but your son is an asshole," Scarlett said.

His mom looked her up and down. "What's your name again?" Marion asked.

"Scarlett."

"Baby, two things I don't play about are my son and husband. You saying he is an asshole is telling me I'm a bad parent to my face. Is that what you're doing?" she sassed and stared at her, waiting for an answer.

Scarlett was stuck on stupid, and I had to say something to cut the tension before it got out of hand. "She didn't mean it like that, Mrs. Michaels."

"Mmm-hmm. I don't tolerate my son being disrespectful, and I'll tell him about himself, but from what I saw, he hasn't had contact with that girl. If he did, we would know."

I heard the door open and felt his presence before he took a step to us. "Baby," he called out.

"Not right now, Joseph," I said.

"She doesn't want to talk to you," Scarlett said, rubbing my back in comfort.

"I think we should give them a few minutes to talk alone," Marion said.

"Jessica, is that what you want?" Scarlett asked.

I nodded, giving her a hug for supporting me. "I'll be fine." They both went back inside the house, and I took a seat on the patio bench.

Joseph approached and squatted in front of me. "Jessica, I know what it may look like, but Natasha and I haven't been together in months," Joseph explained.

"Before we got back together?"

"She was there when we split up, and we hung out a few times."

"Why didn't you pursue anything permanent?" I had to know; my palms were sweaty, and my stomach was turning into knots.

"Because she's crazy!" he said.

My eyes widened in surprise. "How long has she been stalking you?"

"Shit, a few weeks, and I thought it was just her showing up as a coincidence, but too many times, I've calculated that it wasn't just a simple bumping into each other like old friends."

"Did you tell Micah?" I queried. My brother was a cop, so he would be the first person I contacted.

"I didn't think anything of it at the time, but now that

she's showing up at my parents', I have to get him involved." He sighed and stood to sit next to me.

"I think you should."

"You forgive me?" he asked.

"Maybe. It depends."

We leaned back, and he reached around my shoulder and pulled me in close to chest. "On what?" He caressed the side of my cheek.

"You doing that thing with your tongue tonight," I muttered, making small circles on his leg with my finger.

"I'll do more than that." He lifted my chin and pressed a kiss to my lips. He slid his tongue into my mouth, and I sucked on it, then pulled back to bite his bottom lip, feeling a wetness in my panties.

I wanted to go home and make up. "Let's go to my place," I said.

"I thought you were hungry?" he asked.

"I am, but not for food," I growled in his ear, biting the side of his neck gently.

"On one condition."

"What?"

"Talk to your girl and let her know I'm not a man to be played with. Our relationship is not up for discussion with her, or anyone else."

"What are you talking about?"

"You don't see it, Freckles, but she's jealous of what we have. How many times has she commented negatively about me when I'm not around?" he asked. I had to think for a second. Most times, since we'd gotten back together —and even when I was apart from him—Scarlett had to speak about why I shouldn't go all-in with Joseph. "Exactly," he said when I didn't answer.

"Baby, she cares about me and wants me to be happy."

"And I don't?"

"That's not what I'm saying at all."

"Keep your ears open. That's all I can ask from you," he replied and stood, extending his hand for me to take.

We walked back into the house, and everyone was talking, drinking, and eating. I saw Scarlett fussing with Rory in the corner, and I wanted to tell her goodbye, but it looked heated.

"You two look better," Marion said.

"Yeah, we're going to head out and talk some more, Ma," he told her and bent down to kiss her cheek.

"It was nice seeing you both again," I said.

His mom stood from her chair and gave me a hug. "Don't let outside chaos disturb your peace," Marion explained.

I thanked her again and squeezed her hand as we started to walk out.

"Jessica! Wait, where are you going?" Scarlett said.

"Home. I'll call you tomorrow."

"I'll ride with you," Scarlett said.

"You don't have to; Joseph will drive me."

"Really?" She looked offended, and I wondered if Joseph's words were really true. Did my friend really not mean well for me?

"She's good with me, Scarlett," Joseph said, pulling on my hand to keep walking.

Scarlett followed us. "What do you mean, 'she's good'? Your plaything showed up here and wanted to fight my friend."

"No, you invited her," Joseph said.

"Doesn't matter, but you two obviously have something going on, and I am not gonna let you use my friend, too. It's not going to work," Scarlett argued.

Joseph opened his car door, and I sat in the passenger side. He slammed it shut. "Scarlett, I suggest you focus more on what's going on with Rory and you, and less on Jessica and her relationship."

"Rory and I are good," Scarlett snapped.

"Scarlett, I'm just looking out for you," Joseph informed her. I tugged on the back of his shirt to get in the car. He nudged me off. I tried to open the door to step out, and he pushed it close. He walked around the front of the car and jumped in on the driver side. Scarlett stormed off back to his parents' house.

"What do you know exactly?" I questioned because Rory was a hoe. Everybody knew he would never commit to one woman.

"I don't know, baby, but it could be anything when it comes to Rory's crazy ass," he fussed. He started the car and drove off.

* * *

Two days later, I was dressed up in my best business attire with Joseph, Brent, and some of their staff from the real estate company. Angela could not make it because she was too far in her pregnancy to fly, and Emery wanted to stay behind to help with the kids and give her a break.

I had not heard another word from that Natasha chick, and his party planner friend had only called when she needed confirmation on something; otherwise, she had not been back to his office since, and I was grateful for whatever had conjured up this peace in my relationship. Even Eric had stopped badgering me and found some girl to put up with his craziness.

I felt a hand on the small of my back, and I smiled,

looking up at my handsome boyfriend and future-investment-billionaire-in-the-making. The things that he had been doing in his business had inspired me to want to invest in multiple areas, like real estate, small local businesses, and more. Brent had said that he could hook me up with an investment banker and accountant once I got an office set up for my graphic design business. I'd picked up two new clients once I finished Brent and Joseph's logo, and they recommended me to some other friends. Now, I was planning another major logo for a community college sports team.

Scarlett and I hadn't sat down and had a conversation since the blow-up, and I'd tried to call her and get together, but she'd sent me straight to voicemail. I'd promised myself that I would give her until tomorrow before I showed up at her job to talk.

Joseph talked with Brent and another business client, as I listened to the ideas they had for the business. "I want it to be not only commercial, but eventually to bring in agents to handle the housing sector," Joseph explained.

"Brent, are you thinking of starting up a division in L.A.? It's huge for buying and flipping homes," Jeremiah suggested.

"I hadn't thought that far. My wife is about to have our third child, plus my marketing business is booming. This is enough for now," Brent told him. I finished off the rest of the champagne.

"You did the logo and design for all the social media, correct?" Jeremiah asked me.

I nodded. "I did."

"Impressive. You have to give me your card. I have things I'm planning," Jeremiah said.

I opened my clutch purse and removed one of my

business cards, then handed it to him. I stroked Joseph's arm, and he pressed a kiss on my cheek. "The grand opening was a success," I said.

Joseph and Brent looked around at the large crowd in the room. The office was decorated in grey and black. There were TVs on the walls, showcasing the brand name, with commercials playing that had been made by Brent's marketing company. There was a large receptionist desk in the lobby, with the logo I'd created on the wall and the brochures. The building had three levels. Joseph kept an office there, but Brent didn't since his marketing firm's main office was there. All the junior and senior agents had offices. Patty was going to be the office manager part-time, until he could find someone to handle things once business picked up. Currently, they had four clients and did not want to overwhelm themselves right out of the gate.

"It is. You ready to go home?" Joseph gripped the side of my waist, pulling me in close.

"I could go for dinner."

"We can do that." Joseph dipped his head and pecked my lips. Locking our hands together, we walked over and said goodbye to everyone. He slapped hands with Brent, Troy, and my brother.

"Sis, you headed out with this one?" Micah asked.

"Yeah. Have you talked to our parents lately?" I asked.

"I talked to Dad, and Mom was busy with work," Micah recalled.

"Can you do me a favor?"

"What's wrong?" His brows dipped low. He grabbed my elbow, walking me away from Joseph. My brother was a hard-ass, but he protected me, and I knew he always had my back.

"Joseph told me about Natasha."

"How'd that go?"

"She showed up at his parents' house. Scarlett invited her." My chest tightened. My emotions were all over the place. I kept wondering if my friend really had my back.

"Wow, seriously?! She came to his parents' house?!" Micah shouted. I shushed him to be quiet when Joseph looked over at us as he finished talking with Patty. "Let me make some calls," Micah said.

"Great. He met her at Club Escape."

"He told me about her and said they only saw each other a few times. I believe him." Micah slid his hand into his pocket and pulled out his cell phone.

"I believe him, too, but she's obviously in love with him."

"Yeah, but he doesn't feel the same way. Don't go making it more than it is, Jessica." Micah typed away on his cell, glancing up at me.

"Keep me updated, okay?" I replied.

"For sure. Otherwise, you good?" he questioned. I stood on my toes and pecked his cheek.

"Micah, you good, bro?" Joseph questioned. He gave him a one-armed hug and patted his back.

"Yep, just checking in with my sister. Making sure your ass ain't acting crazy," Micah joked.

Joseph held hands out in surrender. "Freckles knows it's all about her."

"Good, and I'm on that Natasha thing," Micah said. Joseph narrowed his eyes at me.

"I wanted him to keep me updated," I said.

"Stop stressing about her, baby," Joseph commented and wrapped his arm around my shoulders.

"Listen to him, Jess. I'll handle it—and call your father," Micah demanded.

I pursed my lips, staring down at my feet. "Fine," I huffed, grabbing Joseph's hand and turning to leave. I heard my brother laughing at me. He knew I would rather not have a family dinner and try to bring my boyfriend around, but I wouldn't get out of it since they never met him the last time we were dating.

Joseph opened the door for me. The cold breeze had me blowing into my hands, and I rubbed them together as we walked to the car. He opened my door. "You seem quiet," Joseph said, shutting my door.

"I'm tired. After finishing this design, getting back with you, and the Scarlett situation, I'm exhausted."

"Well, I'll take you home and work out your problems in the best possible way," Joseph said, lifting his palm to my lips. He released my hand and walked around to the other side, then got in. We pulled out and headed back to my place for the rest of the night.

Chapter 12

Jessica

Being inside Club Escape in a private room a few days later brought out the mystery of it all. There was a masquerade party tonight, and everyone had dressed in their best ball gowns and suits with masks over their faces. We had walked into the bar area and watched couples talking and engaging with each other. They introduced themselves to me and Joseph. They had not seen me since the first time I was there and had wondered what happened to me.

Now, we were displayed on a bed with a mirror on the ceiling, knowing that we could be watched at any time. My heartrate sped up as Joseph did not waste any time before running his tongue across my nipple. I trembled in his hold as I reached out to grab the back of his head and push him even closer.

He nudged my hand away. "No touching," Joseph demanded, moving my hair to the side and kissing along my neck, then my cheek.

I writhed in bed, watching the muscles in his back. I chewed on my lip, arching off the bed as he trailed kisses down my chest to my stomach, swirling his tongue in my belly button. I relaxed my hand on his shoulder, then squeezed, opening my legs further for him. He massaged my feet, then kissed back up my leg to my inner thigh. Our lovemaking had always been intense pleasure; he always made sure that every curve of my body was worshipped, and only then would he relinquish and take his pleasure.

I felt a cool breeze when he separated my lips below. "Beautiful," he whispered.

I tossed my head from side to side, knowing his favorite thing to do was suck me into a deep sleep. "Baby."

"I want you like this every night, baby," he said, blowing on me.

I flinched and tried to move out of his hold. He pushed me back down. He leaned in and lapped up my juices, then gently bit my labia. "Ugh, please, Joseph!" I gripped the sheets, feeling like I was floating on a cloud as his tongue flicked and licked every corner of my pussy. My eyes started to roll into the back of my head. I felt my heart palpitating fast, and my body heating up. He reached over, not taking his eyes off me as he picked up a small ice cube and put it into my mouth to suck on it, then placed it in my pussy. I jumped from the cold pressure and tried to move out of his strong hold. "Oh, my God! I can't... wait."

He shook his head, pushing his face even farther into my core. The loud smacks of him eating me out reverberated through the room. Then he hovered over me and lined his dick up at my entrance. I tried to think of anything to distract myself from coming so early. Something about the way he treated my body made it so that I could not control myself when I was naked for him to devour. His tongue sunk into my mouth, and he captured my lips. He groaned, pushing his weight harder on top of me as his dick found my G-spot on first contact.

"Mmm," I moaned.

"Fuck, you're tight. I can barely hang on without coming," he grunted, pulling back out.

"Stop playing..." I whined, gripping his ass cheeks and forcing him back inside me. We both groaned, and I met his thrusts.

"I love you," Joseph muttered, lifting my leg and putting it over his shoulder to get deeper.

"Ahhh... fuck. This is... ugh." I could not form a clear sentence.

His thrusts sped up. He looked down at our connected bodies and watched as he disappeared in and out. Sweat beads fell from his forehead to my chest. "Ahhh... baby... damn you," he scoffed. I flushed in embarrassment and tried to hide my face in the pillow. He picked my chin up. "Look at me."

I shook my head. "No, I can't!" I simpered loudly.

"Nah-uh. Stay with me here."

"You are too much." I giggled.

"I don't care. Your shit is the best, and I'll fuck somebody up over you." He pulled back, thrusting faster as he panted. Our bodies slapped together. He licked his thumb and played with my nipple, twisting and squeezing.

"Oh, shit! I'm coming, baby!" I screamed, arching off the bed.

He pulled out fast and rolled me over, then slapped me on the ass. "Arch your back."

I got into his favorite position, looking back at him as he put his mouth back on my wet folds, and then an intense feeling came when he stuck his thumb in my ass.

"Ahhh... Joseph!" I screamed. I could not hold out any longer and collapsed on the bed as I squirted.

He continued to eat me out, lifting me again as I trembled in his arms. He pushed back in and pumped two more times, then released inside me. "Never doubt me," Joseph said, kissing the side of my face as he thrusted slowly. I grabbed his thigh and nodded. My eyelids drooped; I felt sleepy and wanted to curl up with a pillow. He lay me down and got off the bed, then walked to the bathroom. My eyelids fluttered as I tried to stay awake.

A few minutes later, he brought a small warm towel to clean first me, and then himself. Then he put it back in the bathroom. Joseph crawled back in bed and grabbed the comforter, and we curled up together in bed to sleep for a few minutes. We had never slept over before—even though this was a private room, and we could stay all morning, I always preferred to be in one of our beds instead.

* * *

The next day, Joseph dropped me back home. I jumped in the shower and fell back to sleep for the next few hours in my bed after thinking about our night. I yawned and pushed a pillow between my thighs; my legs were still sore and wobbly from him working me over in different areas.

My phone rang. "Ugh," I groaned, reaching over to grab my phone off my night table. I answered without looking at the name. "Hello."

"Pumpkin!" Mom said.

"Ma?" I checked the time on the clock and saw that it

was one in the afternoon. I sat with my back to the head-board and wiped my eyes.

"Hey, baby, you hungry?" she asked.

"Huh?"

"Come open the door."

"What?"

"Jessica, focus. Get off your ass and come open the door, child," Mom fussed and ended the call.

I stared at the phone, shook my head, and got out of bed. I grabbed my robe off the chair and slid into my slippers, then headed to the front door of my apartment. I slid the locks back and opened it up. I saw my mom, smiling with bags of food in her hand. I stepped to the side and let her walk into the kitchen with the food. "What are you doing here?" I asked.

Lesley Samuels was the type of person who could kill people with kindness but strike like a snake if they crossed her or hurt her family. She was a retired lawyer and loved to travel with her friends—and lately, her boyfriends, who were half her age sometimes. "I can't come see my daughter?"

My father was more of the comforter in our family. He listened to our problems. Our mom was not the biggest nurturer, but that didn't mean she didn't care. She just had more of a drill-sergeant-like mindset.

"Ma don't start. You know I'm happy to see you."

"Good. Go wash your ass and come out here and eat."

I sighed and turned to stroll into the bathroom. I brushed my teeth and changed into some decent clothes in case she tried to spring something on me, and I needed to be ready to bail myself out. "Okay, so, how was Bora Bora?" I asked as I walked back into the living room and sat at the table. She had a spread of wraps, salads, and fruit laid out. I picked up a tomato and popped it into my mouth.

"Bora Bora was wonderful. I drank, danced, and shopped." She poured a glass of sparkling cider into my cup.

"I'll have to take you up on your offer for a trip next time."

"That'll be wonderful, baby. Now, tell me what has been happening with you. We haven't talked in a month or two."

"That's because you're constantly traveling."

"Yes, but that doesn't mean I'm not there for you."

"I've been fine, plus Micah and Daddy keep me company."

"How is your father doing?"

I picked up a knife, cut a wrap in half, took a large bite, and moaned. The flavors were fresh and inviting, with a hint of spicy seasoning. "Daddy's good. You should call him and check in. You both said you've always been friends."

"We are, and I will. Micah called me a week ago about you dating Joseph again."

"Micah needs to stay out of my business."

She laughed and sprinkled dressing over her chicken salad. "That will never happen. So, how are things with Joseph?"

"We're great. You know, his parents and I get along great, and we've hashed out our problems."

"That's good. What about Eric?"

"Eric's not a thought in my mind." I leaned back in my chair and crossed my legs, taking a sip of my drink.

"Good. I told you that boy was an idiot, and a user. So, Joseph's the one?'

"Yes." I blushed and covered my smile with my hand.

"I'm happy for you, baby."

"Thanks. I thought you'd lecture me about my dating life, but I see you've grown up."

"I'm still your mother. Anyway, how is graphic design?"

"Amazing. I finished a big project for Brent and his company. Then I got recommended to one of Brent's friends. It's a huge opportunity to come up with a design."

"Have you thought about getting an office and hiring more designers to cut the workload down?"

I jumped up and went to the kitchen to grab more napkins. "Eventually, I want to get a building, but I'd prefer to have more clients first."

"Well, you know, I'll give you money if you need it, baby."

"Thanks, but I want to do this on my own."

"How is Scarlett doing? She hasn't called me in forever. Neither has her mother."

"She and I aren't speaking right now. I'm going to try to call her, though."

"Why aren't you talking? That's your best friend from your childhood," Mom said, dropping her napkin on the table.

"I don't want to get into a long conversation. Just some things between us that we need to work out."

"Mmm-hmm."

"Ma, leave it alone."

"Remember, I know when you're not telling the truth. I want to have dinner with you and Joseph before I leave town again."

"Please don't start the interrogation."

"I promise to be on my nicest behavior." She smirked, then winked at me.

We continued eating lunch and catching up for the rest of the day, and then went shopping before she went back to her hotel. She had been living in Chicago since the divorce, and we would often visit my brother, so thinking about her moving back here for good would be a little different but better as a whole for our family.

Chapter 13

Jessica

A month later, Angela had her baby boy. They named him B.J., short for Brent Jr. He was a little chubby-cheeked chocolate drop. We were on a Facetime together, and right now, B.J. was propped up with pillows and looking into the camera, probably wondering who the hell I was, as everyone in their house continued to fawn over him. The girls helped out by taking turns with the kids as much as possible since their daughters wreaked havoc all day and night. They were still getting used to the baby, and sometimes they would cry when he was brought next to them. Granny said it was a territorial thing, and they did not want to share Angela with him.

"Ahhh, he's so cute!" I exclaimed.

"He's my miracle baby," Angela said. Brent came onto the screen and kissed her cheek. Brent had flown right back to L.A. after opening night and stayed close to home —even working from his house when they needed him on certain calls. Overall, he left his business in the hands of his VP.

"Can you sleep through the night?" I asked.

"On and off. Still getting him used to a schedule," Angela remarked, taking a seat on the couch to get comfortable.

"He looks just like Brent."

"I know. I couldn't let my other baby-daddy know, or he'd get jealous," Angela joked. Brent reached over and squeezed her breast. She smacked his hand away and rubbed the soreness. "Such an asshole," Angela grunted.

"Love you, babe!" Brent called out from the background.

"So, tell me. What's been up with you?" Angela asked.

"Working and living life. Joseph and I have been great. No hiccups."

"Did Micah get that situation taken care of?"

"Natasha hasn't shown up anywhere so far. Hopefully, she got the message."

"What about his little decorator girlfriend?" Angela wondered.

I chortled. She was always calling her his "decorator girlfriend". "Taylor hasn't popped up—only calls when she needs him to answer a question."

"Good. We'd hate to have to kick his ass before you get the ring."

"I'm not looking for a ring, girl."

"Please, that boy loves your dirty drawers. He's probably picking one out as we speak."

"Who are you talking to, Angela?" I heard Granny ask.

"Jessica."

"Let me talk to her," Granny said.

I heard kids laughing in the background. "Hi, Granny Lynn."

"Hey, sugar. How are you?"

"I'm doing good."

"When are you coming back to L.A.?" Granny asked.

"Probably not for a while. Busy working and building my portfolio."

"I saw your design on the TV. You got skills, girl." Granny said, sounding like a 25-year-old.

"Thank you. I hope I made you proud."

"Of course, you did. I talked to your mother."

A lump formed in my throat as I waited to hear the news. "She wants to have dinner with Joseph and find out what his intentions are with you."

"That woman is a mess."

"I know, and I told her that's none of her business. You're grown, in your 30s, fucking and suck—"

"Granny! Granny!" I heard shouting from the background, and the phone dropped on the floor. I dropped my head into my hands, chuckling at her going off on them for interrupting her conversation.

"No, we have kids in the room, old woman," Angela fussed.

"These babies don't understand me. Your ass was doing a lot of S-E-X, and that didn't stop you," Granny argued. I was bent over the couch, laughing at the two of them going back and forth, with tears pooling in my eyes.

"Will you please feed your grandchildren and leave me alone?" Angela huffed.

"Give me my baby," Granny said.

"Fine," Angela said in exasperation, then got back on the line. "Hello."

"Girl, that woman is a mess," I said.

"I swear, I wish I could put her in a home, but she's technically only Emery's grandmother, so the place wouldn't allow me to do that without Emery's signature."

"Oh, my God! Angela, tell me you didn't go down to try and sign Granny into a home?" I questioned.

"No, I just called to see if they have openings," Angela mumbled.

"I heard that!" Granny yelled.

"Good!" Angela replied.

"Lord, I have to pray for you two," I said.

"Anyway, have you talked to Scarlett?" Angela questioned.

"I'm meeting her today for lunch. We haven't spoken since his parents' place, and she has been out of town working."

"Okay, well, make sure you get your point across that your relationship is off-limits, and if she's going to be the type of friend who has to comment negatively on everything, then that's a friendship you don't need."

"I will. Let me go; it's getting late, and I told Joseph I would spend the night at his place, but I need to get some work done first."

"All right. Call me tomorrow or whenever you get a chance."

"Thanks. And kiss the baby for me." We said our goodbyes, and I ended the call, then jumped off the couch, grabbed my purse and sweater, and headed out to meet Scarlett for lunch.

* * *

15 minutes later, I parked at the sub shop that we often went to and got out of my car. I shut the door and turned

the alarm on. It was still sunny out, and cars were blasting up and down the street. I opened the door and stepped inside, seeing Scarlett sitting in the corner booth with a drink in her hand.

"Hey." I slid in across the booth from her, placed my purse down, and removed my shades and sweater.

"Hi," she said dryly.

I cocked my neck back in surprise. "I thought we were better than that."

"You tell me, Jessica. Ever since you got with Joseph, you've been different."

"What are you talking about?"

"I'm just surprised you'd allow another guy to come in and dictate your life."

"Joseph is not Eric."

"He probably puts on a good show, but Natasha said they've been talking for a while."

"Wait, have you stayed in contact with her?"

"We've talked a few times. After she was kicked out of the party, I wanted to find out the truth."

"The truth about what?"

"Joseph and her."

I slid my sleeves up, grabbed a glass of water, and took a sip to calm my nerves.

"He's probably unfaithful, Jessica," she continued.

"According to Natasha?"

"Yes. She said they have been going to Club Escape together, and he was talking about them getting serious."

"Listen, you're my friend, and I hope you trust that I know what's best for me, and you'll support me."

"I support you, but when I see you doing the same thing again and falling in love with someone that will hurt you, I have to speak up."

"Joseph has done nothing but be a great, supportive boyfriend. I'm not sure where Natasha is getting her information, but we've been together every day for the past month unless we're working."

"She said he's been seeing some Taylor girl," Scarlett mentioned.

"Scarlett, you're letting this girl come between us, and honestly, it's causing me to look at you differently."

"What are you saying?"

"If you're my friend, then you'll leave it alone."

"Just like that? And if it turns out he cheated?" Her brows raised.

"He's not cheating; the girl is crazy. Taylor is doing the opening of his community center."

"Men cheat; it's in their nature," Scarlett muttered.

"So, you're putting your own issues onto me because your guy can't keep it in his pants?"

"Sorry, Jessica. I'm just worried about you, babe."

"I understand, but we're good."

She changed the subject, talking about some styling contract that she was looking to get hired for with a magazine. I felt something more was going on, but I would not allow her judgment to come between Joseph and I when I was finally happy.

Chapter 14

Joseph

I had just parked and got out of my car at the courtyard to go play ball with the guys for a little bit, and then meet Taylor at the center to do a quick run-through of the events. Rory tossed the ball to me, and I closed the door and lifted my bag over my shoulder as we walked and talked. I continued texting with Jessica, who had told me that tomorrow, she wanted me to have dinner with her family.

Jessica: Me and Scarlett had a fight.
Me: About me?
Jessica: Yeah, and Natasha.

I groaned, annoyed that Scarlett was still bringing up that dumbass girl again. I didn't need any more people in her life to hate. I didn't want her to leave me again.

Me: Micah said he spoke with Natasha.
Jessica: What did she say?
Me: Same bullshit, that I asked for more, which I did not.

Jessica: Time for me to kick her ass?

I chuckled at her response.

"That must be Jessica because you don't laugh at anybody else," Rory said.

"Don't hate."

Me: He told her that if she didn't stop, then he had to get a restraining order against her.
Jessica: Good.
Me: Give Scarlett some time.
Jessica: I guess. Rory has not called her in a month.

"Damn."

"What?" Rory asked, dropping his bag next to Denver. We slapped hands as Micah approached from the other side of the court.

"You haven't called Scarlett in a month?"

"Man, that girl wants to get married and have kids. I'm not looking for that," Rory fussed.

"Did you tell her that?"

"Yeah, when I had her sucking my dick." He grabbed his crotch, and I waved him off.

Me: Rory's here with me now.
Jessica: He's an asshole, babe.
Me: I know.
Jessica: I'll let you go. Call me later for the walkthrough.

I put my phone in my bag and removed my sweatpants. I left my ball shorts on to play a few rounds. "Scarlett is still talking reckless about me."

"Shit, that's not my fault." Rory grabbed the ball out my hand and went to dunk.

"It is, because she thinks I'm like your ass."

"What'd I do?" Rory scoffed, offended at my accusation.

"You're using the girl and leaving her hanging," Micah said.

"That's on her. I never promised rainbows and sunshine," Rory said. He dribbled the ball and went for a three-pointer. I blocked him and tucked the ball under my arm for a second, looking from left to right, then twisting to rebound the shot.

"Rory, you have to admit you're a dog. This is coming from me," Denver said, taking the ball and passing it to me. Micah and I nodded at each other, laughing because Denver was just as bad, but not worse. Denver went back and forth between his baby-mama and the latest groupie he could find whenever he hit the club with Rory.

"At least I don't have a crazy baby-mama on my heels." Rory raised his hand to play defense. We ran up and down half the court, then back up. I jumped to hit a shot, but the ball missed. "You are getting old, man. Can't hit a simple shot," Rory teased.

"You're no better," I countered.

"So, how are things with Jessica?" Rory asked.

"Good. Better than I could have hoped for after all this time."

"Natasha shouldn't be a problem anymore," Micah said, taking the rebound.

"As long as she stays away from Jessica, I'm good."

"Have you been to Club Escape lately?" Denver questioned.

I did not want to answer that question in front of

Micah, since the only time I went back was with his sister. "What's up with you and Scarlett?" I asked Rory instead, stepped in front of him to block him from shooting a three-pointer.

"I don't know. Sometimes, I want to just fuck; other times, she drives me crazy with her wanting commitment," Rory said with a disapproving look on his face.

"Let me ask you a question," Micah challenged, heading to the bench to grab a bottle of water.

"Here goes the biggest man-whore of the group, trying to tell me what I'm doing wrong," Rory joked.

Micah twisted the top off the bottle, gulped the water down, and burped. "You're an ass, Rory. We all know this and still hang out with you, but women need a little more finessing and assurance. Scarlett is sensitive and pretends to have it all together," Micah explained.

Rory shrugged, ignoring his words. The game went on, and we stopped talking about women and dating. Instead, we focused on winning and getting our money back from last time.

I helped Jessica out of the car and shut the door. I fixed my jacket and entwined our hands to head inside. We were going to meet with Taylor to do a walkthrough of what she'd set up. The grass outside was freshly cut, and a new sign had been put out front with our logo on it.

Jessica wanted to go out to dinner tonight, so I promised we would right after, and maybe catch a movie if it wasn't too late.

"Hi, you made it right on time," Taylor said, pushing the door open to let us inside. I stood to the side and let

Jessica go in first. We looked around the entrance. Everything was freshly painted, and the staff was moving around the furniture. "This is the red carpet, where people will come in and take photos." Taylor waved her hand around. A poster of the kids was sitting on top of the reception desk that I'd had installed with security cameras inside and out.

"Did the computers come in yet?" I asked.

"They did, and we had the tables delivered today. I talked to the band," Taylor said, avoiding eye contact with Jessica.

"What do you think?" I asked Jessica, sliding my hand down to her soft ass and cupping it gently.

"You should be really proud of what you've built. I like the different plaques on the wall of the athletes, and where they grew up," Jessica said, walking out of my hold. I was working on getting major athletes to come out and volunteer here and give speeches to motivate the kids. I planned on opening the center for boys and girls from ages 9-18—especially those who weren't doing well in school because of a lack of food and housing. I planned on having an area for parents to volunteer and to help get them back into the workforce.

"Your mother was planning on making cupcakes, and gift bags for the kids with little treats inside. She wanted me to confirm with you." Taylor led us into the gym, where we would have the event since it was largest area of the center.

I walked around and stared at the amount of work that had gone into building the place back up from how it used to be. It was so rundown. No one would have thought that this place could have been brought back to its former glory. "Whatever she wants to do. I'm fine with her making them."

Taylor smiled and started to step closer to me.

Suddenly, Jessica joined us in the gym. "Joseph, this place is huge. I almost got lost."

"You ready to go eat?" I cut the tension.

"You did a great job, Taylor," Jessica announced.

Taylor thanked her, as another member of her staff approached us. "We have the invitations ready to go out if you want to sign off," her assistant Emily said, holding out her iPad.

"Perfect. You want to take a look, Joseph?" Taylor held the iPad out for me.

I looked at the design and smirked, seeing Jessica's branded logo. "When did you do this?" I asked and swung Jessica into my arms.

"What are you talking about?" Jessica asked, running her hands up my arms.

"The design on the invitations. I like what you did."

"I didn't do—" She grabbed the iPad and stared at it. She glanced up at me, and then at Taylor.

"I checked out your website and thought your work was good. So, I picked one of your designs," Taylor mentioned.

Jessica was surprised by the gesture. "Thank you," Jessica said.

"I admire another businesswoman," Taylor said.

Jessica extended her hand for a shake, and Taylor reached her hand out, too. They shook hands.

I finished the walkthrough, and a few minutes later, I escorted Jessica out to dinner at a nice restaurant near Broadway. The waitress brought out menus and poured a glass of water for each of us. The candles were lit, and the dining room was not as crowded, so it was a little more intimate.

"Did I mention you look sexy as fuck tonight?" I asked.

"Hmm, let me think. This is the first time tonight," Jessica said, smirking at me.

"What can I do to make up for not acknowledging how beautiful you look sooner?"

"Oh, I have a few ideas. Maybe I'll create a list for you."

I chuckled and reached over, grasping her hand in mine. I lifted it to place a kiss on the back.

"What do you have an appetite for?" Jessica inquired, lifting the menu and scanning the main courses and desserts. "I'm starving. I want a steak or something."

"I'll get the same. How did everything go with your mom?"

She closed the menu, cupped her chin, and looked into my eyes. "She's thinking of moving here."

"That's good, right?"

"I don't know, Joseph. My mom is very opinionated and thinks everything could be solved if we just listened to her."

"Aren't we having dinner with her and your father?"

"Don't remind me."

"I'll do whatever you want me to do. Just relax tonight, and we'll handle whatever is thrown at you together."

"Thank you." She leaned over the table and puckered her lips. I pecked her twice on the mouth.

The waitress came over to our table. "You guys ready to order?"

"We'll both have the same thing—steak, steamed rice, mashed potatoes, and salad, please," Jessica ordered. The waitress jotted everything down and took our menus away.

I picked up the bottle of red wine and poured a small amount into each of our glasses. "I want to propose a toast."

"All ears."

"I want to say it was a rocky start, but I've learned and forgiven. I've loved and felt loved by you. I thank you for being you." We clinked glasses, and I winked as I took a sip of the wine. "What's the next design project you have coming up?"

"I'm excited about it. I'm thinking of opening an office."

"You should."

"That would probably mean taking on more clients, with all the costs of running a business."

"Do you need my help?"

"Nope. I'm doing this on my own, sir."

"I understand but don't feel like you need to burden yourself when I'm here and have the means to help you."

"I know but I like figuring things out on my own." Jessica pushed her phone in the middle of the table and showed me a few buildings that she had been scouting out to rent.

Chapter 15

Jessica

The waitress brought our meals out 20 minutes later and placed them in front of us. We fed each other and talked. It was nice to be out as a normal couple, without all the craziness of our past mistakes coming between us.

"Jessica!"

I almost choked on my food when Eric called my name. He was standing with a girl who was half-dressed in a skintight bodycon dress, showing off her large breasts, with overdone makeup. Joseph passed me a glass of water, so I could get myself together. I picked up my napkin to wipe my mouth. "Eric, what are you doing here?"

"I could ask you the same thing."

I was visibly annoyed with his presence. The girl clung to him, and her eyes shot daggers at me—even though they had approached us at our table. "I'm having dinner with my boyfriend."

"Is this the guy you left me for?" Eric asked.

I jerked back in shock. "What did you say?" his girlfriend and I said at the same time.

"Cynthia, be quiet," Eric said.

"No, *you* be quiet," Cynthia said. "We're supposed to be celebrating being pregnant, not talking to your ex-girlfriend."

"Eric, please go," I said.

"I want an answer because you lied to me all this time, and I was thinking we could work something out," Eric said to me. I rubbed my temples and popped my neck. This man was crazier than I thought.

"My man, we're trying to have a peaceful dinner together." Joseph started to rise from his seat.

"Joseph, no," I said. "He is not worth it. Please sit down."

"My mother was right about you. Not only are you trash in bed, but you're a stuck-up bitch," Eric muttered. He started to walk away, and Joseph jumped up and grabbed him by his jacket collar.

"Joseph! Stop. He's not worth the punch, baby," I pleaded.

Cynthia tried to push Joseph away, and the security guard of the restaurant approached us to see what was going on. "Sir, you need to let him go and take this outside," the security guard said, and I nodded.

"I want him arrested!" Cynthia shouted.

"Eric started it and came to our table, so if anyone is going to get arrested, it should be him," I said.

"I dare you to say anything else, and I'll kick your ass in front of your girl," Joseph said to Eric through gritted teeth.

Eric opened, then closed his mouth. He held his hands out in surrender, like a little bitch. Now that I thought about it, he always talked a good game but never could back up anything unless it was with a woman.

Joseph removed his hands and reached for my elbow. I grabbed my purse while Joseph paid the bill and we walked out, as Eric started to fuss again behind our backs. "What did you ever see in him?" Joseph asked.

"Blind loyalty."

The valet brought our car around after Joseph passed him his ticket. We stayed outside, curled up in each other's arms. "You coming to my house tonight?" Joseph asked.

"I have work to do, babe."

"We can stop off and grab it, then you can come over to spend the night with me." The car roared up, and he released me to open the passenger-side door. He waited for me to get settled, then walked around and got in. He shut the door.

"If you don't mind me working late, then I'll stay at your place."

"That's what I love about you—your work ethic."

"Um, really, now?"

"Yeah. You put on your glasses, and my shirt, and your big socks, and you get into design-girl mode. Sexy as shit," Joseph teased, and I cackled, shaking my head.

The tub at his place was large and sat two people. I loved when he let me soak for hours and have a moment to myself without any interruptions. Right now, he was off to the guest shower, and I was in his bathroom. I turned on the radio and pinned my hair up, closing my eyes and finishing off a beer while thinking over the months I'd had with him since we made things official. My business was growing, our sex was off the charts, and he was just humble, the complete opposite of what I was used to in a man. I took it for granted. I chuckled, thinking about how I could have ended up with Eric again, pregnant and probably alone because he did not seem to even care about the girl he was with while he got in our face at the restaurant. I hoped she had a good support system and family because more than likely, she would be a single mom.

My phone vibrated. I picked it up and saw a message from my mom.

Mom: Dinner tomorrow night?

Me: Are Dad and Micah going to be there?

I needed to have backup in case she started interrogating Joseph.

Mom: Yes, Jessica. You act like I never met a boyfriend of yours.

Me: This one is serious.

Mom: Then he shouldn't be scared to meet me.

Me: He's not.

Mom:I'll determine that tomorrow.

Me: Don't embarrass me.

Mom: I'm only looking out for your best interest.

Me: Yeah, right.

Mom: Get some rest. Love you, baby.

Me: Love you back.

I closed the message thread and checked if Scarlett had sent anything. We had never had issues between us about men before, and I was worried that this could lead to a bigger issue in the future.I sighed and stood, letting the water out of the tub and grabbing a towel to dry off. I dialed Emery's number to get her opinion on what she thought I should do since more than likely; Angela would just tell me to cut her off.

"Hello," she said, then immediately interrupted herself. "No, J.J., put the game away."

"Hey, Emery."

"Hey, girl. What's wrong? You sound out of sorts," Emery said.

I leaned against the bathroom counter, holding the towel up. "I need some advice."

"What's up?"

"Scarlett and I had a fight."

"What did you fight about?"

"Joseph."

"What about Joseph?"

"She thinks I'm making a mistake and getting in too deep with him."

"Huh."

"I know. She's involved with one of his friends, and things aren't going well."

"So, she's projecting that onto you guys?"

"Yes, but another situation with one of Joseph's exes popped into the equation." I dropped the towel and grabbed a fresh pair of panties out of my bag. I slid my legs inside with the phone between my shoulder and neck.

"Was it a fling type of thing or a serious ex?" Emery questioned.

"You know, I met him in Club Escape."

"Yeah, like an adult club or something, right?"

"He met another girl there, and they played around a few times, and she caught feelings."

"Gotcha. I mean, all I can really tell you is that you need to put yourself first and worry about everything else second."

"I had a feeling you would say that."

"I made the mistake of lying to Jackson early in our relationship, and it took a while for him to trust me again. Then I ended up pregnant and did the same thing by keeping it from him."

"He forgave you."

"He did but having everyone involved in our business wasn't helpful for the growth of our relationship. Angela is a prime example with Brent. We know how long it took her to get right with him," Emery explained.

I recalled the years they spent going back and forth until he dumped her for good. "I hate to lose a friend."

"If she's really your friend, then she would under-stand and support you, not let this other girl that she just met get in her head," Emery said.

"You're right."

"I know I'm right, and Granny said if she needs to come bust somebody on their head, let her know."

We both burst into laughter. I told her that I would call her back later and finished getting ready for bed. I brushed my hair, wiped off my excess makeup, and cleaned my face. I headed to the bedroom and saw my laptop and glasses on top of the bed. I smiled and crawled into bed next to Joseph, then pressed a kiss to his lips. "Thank you, baby."

"Move in with me?" he asked.

I sat up straight in bed and looked at him in shock. "Did you just say, 'move in with you'?"

He reached over and gripped my thigh, peering up into my eyes. "I want you to move in with me, Freckles. I like waking up to your bad breath in the morning," he joked.

I punched him in the arm. "You're such an ass, Joseph. Move, so I can do some work." I tried to remove his hand.

He punched me on my inner thigh. "I'm kidding, baby. I love you, and I know where I want us to go."

"This doesn't have to do with you meeting my parents for dinner tomorrow?"

"No, I've thought about this for a while. I appreciate you thinking your parents intimidate me, baby, but I'm good." Joseph pecked my lips and leaned back on the bed with his arms behind his head. He was wearing pajama bottoms and no shirt.

"Okay."

"Okay?"

"Yes, I'll move in with you." I bent down and sucked on his bottom lip. I ran a hand down his chest to his stomach, then to the line of pubic hair around his shaft.

"See, you're starting stuff you can't finish," he groaned and removed my hand.

I giggled and lifted his chin to tap his nose with my finger. "Be a good boy."

"I'll think about it." He grabbed the remote and turned the channel to ESPN, which had the latest football game on.

I picked up my laptop and went through the early designs of my next logo and social media project for a client. We stayed like that for hours, until after 1 AM. I turned my computer off and picked the remote out of his hands. I shut the TV off, curled up next to him under the covers, and went to sleep in his arms.

* * *

After waking up to breakfast in bed the next morning, I had to leave to meet up with a potential client about using my services. He was a music executive, and he wanted me to create designs for his label. I was super excited to get my footing in the entertainment industry. He'd found me on social media and emailed about meeting up to do some work for his artists and potentially for his other businesses that he had a hand in. His office was close to Joseph's, so I told Joseph that I would meet him there after, and we could drive to my parents' place and leave my car at his shop.

I parked and grabbed my iPad and purse, then checked in with the front desk.

"Jessica, right?" the receptionist asked.

"Yes, Jessica Samuels. 11:30 appointment."

She typed in my name and printed an ID badge and parking validation, then lifted the phone to make a call to her boss. "She's here, sir. Yes, I'll send her right up."

I hoped to seal the deal without any massive demands; some artists wanted full control and never let the designer flow with their creative juices.

"You're all set," the receptionist announced. "Go through those doors. That's the conference room. He'll meet you there."

"Thanks." My heels clicked against the floor. I was wearing my best pantsuit, with my hair in a tight bun on top of my head. I had not worn as much makeup; I wanted to keep it pretty clean and simple since it was more business casual.

"Jessica! Thanks for coming," Scott Turner said, standing at the conference room doors. He reached out for a handshake.

I gripped his hand gently. "Thank you for having me." I walked into the room and took a seat across from him and the other staff. We all exchanged pleasantries, and I pulled out my iPad and business cards.

Scott shut the door and walked to the head of the conference table. He took a seat. "As you know, I have a roster of 10 artists," Scott mentioned, turning his laptop toward me and showing me the company's website.

"I do."

"We have a variety of musical genres: pop, rock, R&B, and classical. I want to revamp our website, and the artists' pages," Scott explained.

"When do you want to have this done?" I was taking notes and swiping through his website, looking at what they had so far.

"The timeline is up to you. I want to make sure we have it right, and that it's not rushed. I have plans to start up a film division, and if everything works out, we could collaborate even more. Can you take on more work right now?"

I tapped my pen against the table and thought about what I had coming up for the future. My dream was to start on a smaller scale and grow as a brand in the graphic design industry. Bringing my touch and style into the music and film industries would put me at the highest level, selecting who I wanted to work for, instead of just taking any project that came my way. "Let me show you some samples first." I turned my iPad around and held it up for all three of them to look at. I scrolled to each design and explained the concept. "This would be your main company logo; we could do it in lighter grey or black. I think that using the same base color you're known for is good."

"Does this include artist social media pages? We'd even think of hiring you to manage the upkeep monthly," Scott stated.

I fell silent; this was even bigger than I'd imagined. Running all their pages meant I would need to hire staff, which meant I would need more money.

"What are you thinking about?" his coworker asked.

"The first estimate didn't include the management of all the sites, so I'd need to go back in and recalculate," I explained.

"Money is no object," Scott said.

"Then I'll get a final figure over to you later today, once I've made some adjustments."

"Sounds good. And can you tack on the film division? You'd be starting from scratch with that one," Scott informed me.

"Did you want me on the management side of it, as well?"

"Definitely. We need all hands on deck, and if you're our main resource, then I know we can have things done in a timely fashion. You came highly recommended," Scott said.

"By who?"

"We rented this building off J&B real estate," Scott told me. That meant Joseph had sent my information through a referral.

"Well, I'll be sending you a follow-up email with all the details soon. Thank you, Scott."

He walked me out of the office, and I waved to the other two in the room, then left my business card with Scott and hopped in my car. I dialed Joseph's number on my way to his office.

"What's up, sexy?" he asked.

"I got the job!" I screamed excitedly.

"I had no doubt."

"Did you really?"

"My baby is not only sexy but smart as shit," Joseph said. I had never felt so much support, validation, and encouragement from a man. It was nice to have someone who had my back through everything. "Where are you?"

"I'm leaving Scott's office now, heading to you."

"Cool, hurry up. I miss you."

"You just saw me this morning at breakfast."

"That was a quick breakfast, and you dashed out of there."

"Yeah, because you wanted me on my back with my legs open," I joked.

He chortled. "I was hungry," he replied.

I shook my head. "Anyway, I'll see you soon. I'm not far from you."

"Drive safe, baby."

"I will," I said and ended the call. I stopped at a red light. I turned the music up a little and tapped my hand against the steering wheel, listening to Mariah Carey. I was in a such good mood. I promised myself not to let my mother stress me out at dinner later.

Finally, I arrived at Joseph's office, grabbed my things, and hopped out of the car. I headed in and stopped to talk to Patty. "Someone looks like they're having a good day," Patty said, passing a receipt to the woman ahead of me in line.

"I just left a business meeting."

"Oh, Joseph told me about that. How did it go?" Patty thanked the woman, then sat in her chair and sipped on her coffee.

"It went great. They want me to manage on top of designing the website and social media pages for their artists."

"You're doing big things, Jessica. I'm so proud of you."

"Thank you. Is he in there?"

"Yes—and alone. Don't be too loud," she chided and winked at me.

I opened his door and stepped inside, hearing him on the phone. I dropped my things on the couch and stepped around to his desk, sitting on top of it and waiting for him to finish. "We can have it painted and cleaned in a week," Joseph mentioned. I placed one leg between both of his, and he threw a lustful stare at me. "How many cars? Okay... yeah. 3000. Talk soon." Joseph finished his call and gripped my leg, then parted my thighs.

"How was work?" I tilted my head up and poked my lips out for a kiss.

"Boring. I missed you, baby."

"I wasn't gone too long."

"For me, you were. And then you show up here, wearing this damn pantsuit." He inspected my jacket.

I giggled at the frown on his face. "Stop being mean. I'm not doing anything with you in your office today, anyway."

"Why not?"

"I have work today, and so do you."

"I can take a day off."

"That's *you*. Besides, I want to get this up and going, plus search for some rental offices online."

"I told you to let me give you a place."

"No, I'm doing it on my own. Focus on your business, and I'll focus on mine."

"Fine."

"Thank you, sir." I pressed a hard kiss on his lips. He groaned and tried to push me onto my back. "You are too much."

"Well, you shouldn't look so damn good today."

"It's a pantsuit."

"Shit, I know, and your ass is sitting just right. Come here and turn around," he said. I slapped his hand away and laughed. He grumbled and sat back in his chair, continuing to work, while I worked on my iPad and made some phone calls.

Chapter 16

Joseph

Jessica's mother cooked a large meal for us. I was starving after working a long day and catching up on new business that I had been neglecting for the past few weeks. I held a bouquet of flowers in one hand and Jessica's hand in the other as we stepped up to the front door of her father's house. It was weird to have dinner at his house with his ex-wife, but Jessica said they got along well as friends, so it should not be a problem.

She knocked on the door. It swung open, and Micah stepped to the side to allow us through. I shook hands with him. "How is she?" Jessica asked.

"Not too crazy," Micah joked.

We shook hands. He hugged his sister, and I let her go, so we could walk farther into the house. It was just like she mentioned—a modest, one-story, stone-and-brick home.

Her father came out of the kitchen, drinking a beer, with a woman behind him, fussing about him not dressing up. "I told you this was an important dinner, Darren."

"I told *you* that I'm fine with what I'm wearing, Lesley!" her father called out.

Her mom looked young, and she was the same height as Jessica, or maybe an inch or two shorter. She had the same light brown skin and curly hair. She smiled when she noticed Jessica and held her arms out for a hug. Jessica walked into her arms and pulled back. I pushed the flowers forward for her to see, and she took them into her hands and smelled them. "Lilies are my favorite," she said and waved for us to take a seat on the couch.

"Mother," Jessica chastised her.

"Joseph Michaels, nice to finally meet you," her mother said, reaching out to grip my hand.

"Nice to finally meet you, as well."

"You've hung out with my son, and I assume you have met my husband."

"*Ex*-husband," Darren said.

Lesley rolled her eyes. "Shut up, Darren," Lesley said, releasing my hand.

"Not tonight, please," Jessica said.

"Listen, the food is ready," Micah said.

"Yes, come on in, so we can eat," Lesley announced and led everyone to the dining room table. It was set for four. I held a chair out for Jessica first, then her mother. "So, Joseph, I hear you're a business owner?" Lesley questioned.

"Yes, ma'am."

"Tell me what you do."

"No interrogating, Lesley," Darren said.

She waved off Darren and picked up a plate to pass around the meatloaf.

"I have a detailing shop, and other investments," I explained.

"Does this detailing shop make good money? I mean, my baby deserves the world." Lesley lifted her napkin and placed it on her lap. She cut into her food and took a bite.

"Oh, my God..." Jessica sighed, exasperated. "I'm not doing this with you. Joseph doesn't need to answer these questions."

"Baby, it's fine," I said.

"See? He knows how to handle himself," Lesley said.

"I'm very well-established, Miss Lesley," I replied.

"What about this Natasha girl?" she asked.

The entire room went silent, and I glared at Micah for telling her my business. "It wasn't me, man," Micah said.

"Don't look at him, I'm a former attorney. I had you checked out." Lesley informed.

"What?!" Jessica cried. "Ma, really?! That's crazy!"

"I'm kidding. Relax. I overheard Micah talking on the phone about it. I like you, Joseph, so welcome to the family," Lesley joked.

"Thanks."

"What do your parents think about my baby?"

"They love her."

"Good. We'd hate to have to make them disappear," Lesley joked, winking at me.

"Ignore her. She thinks she's in the mafia or something," Darren said.

"Darren, if you don't shut up—" Lesley barked. They went back and forth for a few minutes, and Jessica, Micah, and I burst into laughter at the two of them.

"For two people who got divorced because you're so opposite, you still seem to keep talking to each other," Jessica mentioned.

"Your father's crazy, Jessica," Lesley said.

"Funny, you didn't say that last night when I had your legs above your head," Darren said.

Micah and Jessica both spat out their food. "Please tell me you're joking," Jessica said.

"Talk to your mother," Darren replied.

"Your father was good for some things, Jessica. What can I say?" Lesley shrugged.

"I think I'm going to be sick," Jessica gagged.

"Are you two getting back together?" Micah wondered.

Darren and Lesley looked at each other and smiled. "Yes," they both answered at the same time.

The laughter and joking went on for the rest of dinner, and I got to know her parents more. We looked at old photo albums of Micah and Jessica together. We even played card games. Lesley was on my team, and we won a few rounds of Spades. The entire night flowed well.

* * *

Once we came back to the house after dinner, we showered and washed each other as we kissed and made promises to each other. Our lives were becoming more and more entangled as a couple.

I took her hardened clit into my mouth as she squirmed on the bed. Her soft moans further pulled at my heart and caused my dick to stand at attention. "I can't wait to have you in my arms every night," I whispered as I slid a second finger across her swollen lips.

"Joseph!" She bit her bottom lip, and we made eye contact. The lust in her eyes told me this was home for her. I planned on surprising her at my parents' anniversary party. I would not expect her to jump into marriage right away, but I had to know if she was open to the idea. "Keep going..."

I grasped my shaft, stroking it up and down, teasing her for a few minutes by not pushing it in. She whimpered with a flushed face. I squeezed her plump breasts and leaned down to flick my tongue across them, going back and forth between them, giving them soft bites and caresses. I could feel her pussy getting wetter and wetter for me. "You ready for me?"

She nodded, staring back at me.

"God, you're beautiful, baby," I said, sinking deeper into her love canal.

"Joseph!" she screamed as I pumped in slow thrusts, keeping my pace and using my thumb to play with her nipples. "I want to taste him, Joseph," Jessica moaned in a daze.

I bent down and nibbled on her lips and abruptly yanked out of her and stroked myself. "Come suck him."

Jessica got onto her knees, and I lay flat across the bed. She took me deep in her throat as I gripped the back of her head and thrusted my hips. She locked eyes with me. "Like this?" She popped my dick out of her mouth, smearing the precum over the tip. She stuck her tongue out, capturing my seed.

I pinched her nipple with one hand and guided her movements. She tightened her lips, and I felt myself about to explode. I squeezed my eyes shut; my head fell back as her hands grasped my legs. I felt my nut rising. "Ahhh!" I groaned, pumping faster into her mouth as she drained me. I stared down at her as she started gagging. I tried to pull back some. Saliva mixed with my come and dripped down her chin.

"I'm not done." Jessica grinned, straddled my waist, and eased down onto my dick.

I arched off the bed as she placed her hands on my chest and rode me with her head thrown back, and her eyes closed. "Baby," I wheezed, feeling her draining me dry.

"Fuck! So good, baby."

"Take this shit!" It was indescribable, and I thought I saw stars from the way her pussy tightened around me.

"Ugh! Yes!" Jessica cried out, and I filled her up with my seed. She collapsed on my chest, and I continued to thrust, as my orgasm was right behind hers. Our soaked bodies lay on the bed, and we could not move from the tiredness of fucking in every angle tonight. "I love you," she said.

"I love you more," I said, pulling the blanket over us and falling into a deep sleep.

Chapter 17

Joseph

The center opening was two days later, and I had to make sure everything was set up with the planner. Plus, my parents' anniversary party was the next day, and I planned on surprising them with a trip to the Bahamas as a gift. Working at the shop and trying to handle a relationship, on top of my responsibility with the center, and my investments with the real estate company, had kept me pretty busy. I made a promise to myself and Jessica that I would relax more and let things progress on their own.

I was in the shower after a long night of fucking my woman to prepare to devote my time to my dream of getting this community center up and running for the kids. Jessica's brother was coming by with a few of his officer friends to help out. We'd become cool through her, and he'd offered to come down and devote some time to mentoring the kids in the community.

I stood in the mirror and stared at my reflection while drying off. I smiled when I saw my baby come into the bathroom, only wearing my t-shirt.

"Good morning." Jessica wrapped her arms around my waist from behind and kissed me on my back.

"Morning. How'd you sleep?" I dropped the towel on the counter and stared into her eyes through the reflection in the mirror.

"Perfect. Do you need any help today?" Jessica came around to my front and lifted herself onto the counter.

I stepped between her legs, gliding my hands up her thighs, then underneath her shirt to her waist. "No, it shouldn't take long to check in with Taylor and be back here for dinner."

"Okay. I have a little work to catch up on, but I'll finish moving in today." She pressed her lips against my cheek.

"Call some of your girls over and order dinner on me."

"Are you sure? I know you and Scarlett aren't the best of friends."

Scarlett was not my favorite person, but she was better than some of her other friends, who didn't support her dreams. "She's fine. But are we still down for my parents' anniversary party?"

"Yep. I'm a little nervous since all your family will be there."

"You've met my parents, and they love you. That's all that matters, babe." I helped her down, and she walked over to turn on the shower. I stood back with my arms crossed, leaning against the sink. She removed her shirt, and all her sexy curves made a reappearance. They caused my shaft to grow under the towel wrapped around my waist.

"I know, but this is your entire family and cousins." Jessica wrapped her hair in a high bun before stepping into the shower and closing the door.

"Stop worrying. You're my girl, and no one is going to change that. Not your ex, not my family."

"And Taylor!" she shouted from the bathroom.

I waved her off and stepped into my bedroom. I dropped the towel and grabbed a pair of boxers out of my drawer. I walked to my closet and picked out a pair of jeans and a t-shirt since it was early in the day, and the event would not be until 5 PM. I had time to run some errands and check in with my parents.

I heard the shower stop 10 minutes later. I zipped up my pants and stuck my feet in my new Jordans when my phone beeped. I grabbed it off the corner of the TV and saw a message from Taylor.

Taylor: Everything is running smoothly.

Me: Great. I am stopping over in a few minutes.

Taylor: Perfect! Can't wait for you to see.

Me: Do I need to bring anything else?

Taylor: Just you... ;)

"Who is that?"

I closed my phone, turned, and licked my lips at Jessica, who was standing in front of me and drying her hair with a towel. "Taylor."

"Is everything okay for the opening?"

"Everything is good; don't worry." I laid my hands on her waist, pulled her against my chest, and kissed her.

She stood on her toes and wrapped her arms around my neck. She opened her mouth, and my tongue slid inside. I massaged her ample ass. She pulled back. "I'm excited for you, baby."

"Thank you. You should be proud of yourself, as well."

"I am. And thank you again for the opportunity. I know we started off rocky after our first meeting."

Jessica knew how I felt about being played with, her indecisiveness, and keeping me at arm's length. I would not rehash the past. As long as we loved each other now and were committed to making our relationship work, that was all that mattered. "You deserved it. After I saw the logo for the real estate business, I didn't want anyone else but you." I stepped back and grabbed my wallet and keys off the dresser. I smacked her on the ass as I headed out of the bedroom.

"Don't forget to call me if you need anything!" she yelled from the bedroom doorway as I walked downstairs and out of the house.

"I will." I locked the door behind me, hit the lock on my key fob, and jumped in my car. I set my seat back to my level since Jessica had been using it to drive around in while she was moving in yesterday. I turned the radio up as J. Cole blasted over the airwaves, and I thought about how things were finally in the right spot for me, personally and professionally.

It didn't take long after getting off the freeway to make it to my destination and park. I hopped out and saw the press already lined up, and some of the kids outside with their parents. They ran toward my car, and I honked my horn in greeting, then parked.

"Mr. Michaels, this looks cool!" one of the little boys said. His name was Jeffrey, and he was being raised by his aunt since his parents passed away in a car accident. She'd struggled with him for a while, until I came along and kind of mentored him with his schoolwork and after-school activities. Now, he was more attentive and less disruptive in class.

"Thanks, Jeffrey. Where's your aunt?" I put a hand on his shoulder and brought him close to my side.

"Over there." He pointed, and I saw his Aunt Lisa, talking to another facility worker. Everyone I'd hired was wearing a shirt with the center's logo on it.

"Cool. Let's go open the center and have some fun."

"Yes!" Jeffrey cheered, clapping his hands.

I walked up to Taylor. "Taylor, are we ready?" I asked.

"Yes, sir. Ready when you are," Taylor mentioned.

"Perfect. Let's get the show on the road."

"Mr. Michaels! Mr. Michaels!" the reporters called out.

"I'm not going to give a long speech; that's not my style. I will just say that I am grateful to the people who donated their time and resources to bring the facility together. This was built out of love for the community and for the kids. I hope it continues to be a safe place for everyone," I said.

Taylor passed me a large pair of scissors, and we cut the ribbon on the door. Everyone clapped, and Jeffrey hugged my legs. Then Lisa approached and hugged me, as more families started to cry in appreciation. I opened the door for everyone to walk inside, and we led them to the red carpet to take photos, then over to the gym, which had food buffets, music, and games set up.

I saw Micah coming in my direction with a few of his cop friends in uniform. "Great turnout," Micah said.

"Thanks. I'm still shocked but happy about everything."

"Is Jessica coming?"

"She should be pulling up soon."

"We booked Natasha in jail the other night. She popped up at the shop, causing problems," Micah informed me.

"Like what?"

"She tried to break into your shop. Denver was leaving and saw her," Micah said.

"He didn't say anything to me."

"Because he knew you had a lot going on right now. Cut him some slack," Micah replied.

"That girl is crazy."

"Yep, she started talking about you being her husband, so she had a right to the building."

"Damn."

"Club Escape girls ain't no joke," Micah teased. I pushed him away from me and flipped him off.

Jessica stepped into the gym, with her parents behind her. "Hey, baby," Jessica said.

"You good?" I kissed her cheek.

"Yeah, just had to run a few errands," Jessica responded.

"This is nice, Joseph," Lesley said.

"Thank you, Miss Samuels."

"Oh, call me *Mrs.* Samuels."

My eyes widened in shock.

"Yep, they went to the courthouse and got remarried," Jessica said.

"Really, Pop?" Micah asked.

"What? Your mother just has something that I can't resist," Darren said.

"That's right, baby." Lesley grinned and gripped his arm.

"Get comfortable, everybody, and have fun," I said.

I introduced Jessica to Jeffrey and Lisa and showed them the different games and photo booths that we had set up for the kids to enjoy themselves. I conducted a tour of the computer room and field outside, where we would have sports teams: soccer, football, golf, and basketball. My goal was to make the kids well-rounded in everything to build their confidence.

An hour later, we all sat at the tables, eating, playing games, and talking with the kids about what they wanted to do in the future.

"I want to be like Mr. Michaels," Jeffrey said.

"Keep working in school and listen to your aunt," I said. "You'll get there."

"Yes, sir," Jeffrey replied and ate his hot dog.

Jessica smiled, and I leaned over to peck her lips. I watched as she talked with her parents and brother for the rest of the afternoon. I knew in my heart she was the woman for me.

Chapter 18

Jessica

I finished putting away the last of my things in Joseph's apartment. I had already called and told my landlord that I was moving out, and he was going to let me out of my lease early. I hung the last picture of me and my family on the wall in the hallway and pushed the trash into the corner for Joseph to take out when he got home.

Scott had told me that he would get back to me sometime today about my proposal for the design fees. Today was not only a huge day personally, but also professionally since my paperwork to form an LLC had come in the mail, and I could officially start the steps of getting a business account and continuing to research rental property.

I picked the towel off the counter and wiped my face, then went to the sink and washed my hands. I started making myself some lunch, taking out a salad, leftover pasta, and bread. I turned the radio on to keep me entertained since today was all about cleaning and working.

The doorbell rang. I put the pasta down, turned to

head to the front door, and unlocked it. I saw my mother and Marion both there together. "This is a surprise."

"Can we come in?" Mom asked.

"Um, I'm in the middle of cleaning; you have to excuse the mess." I stepped aside and allowed them to enter, then shut the door.

"We talked to Joseph, and he told us you were here unpacking," Marion said.

"I am—or I was. I just put the last picture up, and now I'm cleaning and cooking lunch."

"The place is coming along great. I'm glad you're putting a little more color in here," Marion said, running a hand across the throw blanket on the black couch.

When I first saw his apartment, it was very bachelor-type. Over time, he started to add a little more color, and he was allowing me to have free reign and make changes now that I was moving in, so we would both be comfortable.

"Have a seat," I said.

Mom and Marion sat on the couch together. I took the chair and tucked my feet under my legs. I was dressed in a long sweater and shorts, with my hair pulled up in a ponytail.

"So, now that your father and I are back together—" Mom started to say.

"How long will it last until you get bored and want to travel?" I interrupted her.

"He's going to travel with me, and we talked this time, so stop worrying. I won't get hurt."

"I'm not worried about *you* getting hurt." My gaze lingered on her.

She gave a curt nod in my direction. "I deserve that,

but we've grown, and we've both changed in a lot of ways," she explained.

"Okay, I support you both, and whatever makes you happy," I said.

"Well, I was hoping you and Joseph would be interested in going on a couples' trip with me and your father, plus Marion and her husband."

"Right now, I'm busy with work; things are taking off fast. I really don't have time to take a trip, Mom."

"Honey, if you work all the time and not live your life, you'll burn out," Marion said.

"I hear you, and I do plan on taking some time off, but the deal I just secured is finalized soon, and I need to hire support staff."

"Keep us updated either way," Mom replied. "Have you talked to Angela since she had the baby?"

"She called me the other day on Facetime, and the baby was awake."

"Time for you and Joseph to start thinking about a baby," Mom threw out there.

"Please do not start with that; we just moved in together. Give us a break." I pinched the bridge of my nose.

"Girl, I was married with two kids and working as a lawyer by the time I was your age. Life moves fast," Mom informed me.

"Well, look at the time," I said. "I need to finish cleaning and running some errands before Joseph gets home. Nice talking to you both."

"You're not slick, little girl," Mom blurted out. "Kicking your own mother out!" She stood.

Marion chuckled and hugged me as I escorted them to the door. "Love you both." I waved goodbye to them and shut the door, then leaned against the back of it and released a long-held breath. "Parents," I grumbled.

* * *

Once I showered, I finished working and making calls. Scott informed me that I was all set, and they approved the fee. I grabbed a bottle of champagne at the local store around the corner after I got gas, then headed to meet up with Joseph at the shop. I wanted to celebrate with him first, before anyone else—even though I had not heard from Scarlett in a while, and I was hopeful that we could mend our friendship and celebrate together, too.

The door was pushed open and Rory stepped out. "Jess, you look good, girl." Rory gave me a hug.

"Thanks. Is it busy there?"

"Not really. He's about to wrap up and head out to grab food, then head home," Rory mentioned.

"I guess perfect timing for me, then."

"Yeah."

"Hey, have you talked to Scarlett lately?"

"Not really—unless we're fighting about something. That girl is crazy, and I'm trying to not block her ass." Rory gestured to his phone.

"If you see her, let me know."

"For sure." Rory walked off, got in his car, and left. I shook my head and wondered what women saw in him. He was the biggest dog and only used women for sex, and they kept falling for it, like my best friend had.

"Hey, baby." Joseph strolled in from his office.

"I was trying to surprise you." I grabbed his chin and kissed him. He cupped my ass and pulled me in close as we moaned into each other's mouths.

"Stop being nasty in the reception area," Patty demanded, shooing us away.

I giggled and pulled back, wiping my lipstick off his mouth. "Sorry."

"What's the champagne for?" Joseph questioned.

"I closed the deal with Scott." I grinned and held the bottle up.

"Congrats, baby. That means I can retire and become a house husband," he joked.

"Well, we are a long way from being that rich."

Patty leaned over the desk and held out three cups. I let Joseph pop the bottle open and pour some champagne into each cup. "To the best woman I know. She not only drives me crazy with her sexy mind, but also the love she has for her friends and family, and her determination. You deserve this win." Joseph kissed me one more time, and we all said cheers and gulped the alcohol down. "How about I take you out to dinner with me?"

"I'd like that. Patty, you want to come?" I asked.

"No, you two celebrate alone. Happy you both finally got it together. You almost gave me a heart attack," Patty chided.

"Call me if you need anything, Patty. I'll keep my phone on." Joseph threw his arm around my shoulder and walked out of his office. We headed to his car. It had become a habit to leave my car at his office and ride with him whenever I showed up, so it was not a big deal when his employees saw it outside. I planned on celebrating with a hot meal and a hot bath, followed by toe-curling orgasms all night long.

Chapter 19

Joseph

The place was decorated exactly how I'd pictured it: cream-colored drapes, and pictures hanging on the walls, with a photobooth set up for people to take pictures with different props. I was glad to have it at the center that we'd just opened. Seeing the entire community come out and help celebrate my parents meant a lot to them and me. It showed how much our presence impacted everyone around us. I even had my parents' favorite band come out and play for them. The Charlottes were an old-school R&B group that played soulful music when I was younger. Every Sunday, my parents danced in the kitchen together, and I did not know at the time how much love radiated from them.

"I have to give it to you, nephew. This party is every-thing," Uncle Kane said, holding a beer in his hand.

I shook hands with him and leaned over to give my Aunt Josephine a kiss on her forehead. "Thanks, Uncle. You look gorgeous as always, Auntie."

"Thank you, baby. Jessica, your dress is beautiful," Aunt Josephine said.

Jessica ran a hand down her dress. "Thank you, Mrs. Michaels," Jessica replied.

"Please call me 'Auntie'. You're a part of the family now," Aunt Josephine said, leaning against my uncle's side.

"The place looks good. You really did what you said you'd do," Uncle Kane said.

I nodded and glanced over at Jessica, who was smiling up at me in admiration. It was because of her that I'd felt the push to complete the project. Having her work on the logo had kept her in my presence, so we could work on rebuilding our relationship.

Her hair was down, flat-ironed, and parted in the middle. Small diamond earrings framed her freckled face, and she wore my favorite lipstick on her thick pink lips, which drove me crazy. I wanted to bite on her bottom lip and pull it between my teeth as she moaned in my ear for me to take her now. I knew it was not time for that because we had just gotten here and needed to make our appearance for at least an hour before skipping out.

"Have you seen my parents?" I asked, coming out of my lust-filled state.

"Yeah, they were talking to some friends near the photo booth," Uncle Kane said.

I took off with Jessica to see them. We headed in the direction of the photo booth and saw the commotion a mile away. I shook my head, as I couldn't hold my laughter in any longer.

"Oh, my God! Who invited them?" Jessica remarked, letting my arm go. She put her hands on her hips and furrowed her eyebrows.

"Hey, Joseph!" Granny Lynn yelled. "I told your parents I wouldn't miss this for the world." She was posing in Pops' lap. The two of them looked like teenagers.

"Hi, Granny. What's up, Pops?" I stretched my arm around my mother's shoulders, and she pressed a kiss to my cheek.

"Jessica, close your mouth, little girl," Granny commented.

"Is Angela here?" Jessica ignored her statement, looking around the room.

"I invited them," I said.

"She's here. Plus, Emery, Jordan, and Jackson flew in with us," Granny said. Jessica's shoulders relaxed.

"Jessica, we've been long-time friends with the Stone family," my Mom said. Granny smirked, and Jessica watched her closely as she stood to dance when the music started to play.

"Baby, stop worrying. They won't embarrass you too bad," I joked.

Jessica sucked her teeth and rolled her eyes as my parents burst into laughter. "Granny is always getting in everybody's business," Jessica blurted out, pointing at Granny as she shimmied, trying to learn one of the latest dances moves from my younger cousin. I had never met a woman as lively as Granny, and I appreciated her honesty. "That woman is a menace." Jessica pushed her hair behind her ears and took a drink off a tray when a waiter walked up to us.

"Party people, what's going on?" Angela waved her hands in the air, and Brent hugged her around the waist. I slapped hands with him and introduced Angela to my parents.

"You could have come alone, without the crazy woman," Jessica whined.

Angela gave her the side-eye. "Nobody runs that old lady. Just ignore her and get drunk; that's what I do." Angela looked off into the crowd. I enclosed Jessica in my arms and pecked her on the lips, then buried my face against her neck.

"Bro, you see the amount of press that showed up at the opening?" Jackson asked Brent.

"It was massive," Brent explained. "The kids loved being there. I'll make plans to come up here and volunteer when I can."

"I appreciate you guys' support," I said. "Seeing my family and friends come together today is great."

"Baby, I'm going to grab something to eat," Jessica said. I released my hold on her, and she walked off with Angela.

"What's your next step?" Jackson questioned.

"Step about what?" I asked. He pointed at Jessica. I shoved my hands in my pockets. "I don't know. We've gotten even closer, and I don't want to scare her off."

"You two have come a long way, but I think she's in a better space and open to the idea of marriage," Brent replied.

"If you both had to do it over again, would you change anything?"

"Probably not. We've all been there with these women. You just had to take a little longer with your girl," Brent said.

I chuckled and watched Granny Lynn steal food off Angela's plate. "She does take after the Stone women—even though she's not related."

"Plus, look at her mom. You have that to look forward to when she gets older."

I shook my head at him. "You just ruined the moment, man."

"What are you three over here gossiping about?" Granny Lynn asked.

"Are you having fun?" I asked.

"Don't try to change the subject on me," Granny said.

"Granny, is it true you almost shot some lady who tried to dance with Pops?" Jackson asked.

"Hell yeah. Cybill's old ass thought she was slick and tried to go on some matchmaking thing with my husband."

"Wait, old people be having these types of problems?" Brent joked.

"You better ask around, son. Granny still got it, baby." Granny snapped her fingers and twirled. All three of us burst into laughter.

The whole family was crazy, and I could not wait to marry Jessica and have our own children, then see how they were with Granny Lynn. I looked off at the dance floor and watched Jessica and Angela, dancing with my parents and laughing while pointing at me. It was the best feeling in the world to have everything I wanted and needed in one room.

Chapter 20

Jospeh

Eight **Months Later**
I watched as Jessica walked out from the back of the boat toward the deck, wearing the black dress I had laid out for her earlier. Since the party, we'd been riding high, working through our busy schedules and hanging out with our respective families. So, I decided to surprise her with a mini-vacation on a yacht that I'd rented from one of Brent's business associates. It was going on 8 PM; the sun was going down, and candles were burning on the table. The little black box that I was hiding was itching to be revealed, and I couldn't wait to see the surprise on her face.

"What do you think?" She twirled in front of me.

I extended my hand for her to take and pulled her in close. Her dress was long, with spaghetti straps, and a small V-neck showing just a hint of cleavage. "I think you get more beautiful by the second."

"I bet you say that to all the girls." She laughed. I cupped both sides of her face, leaned down to press a kiss to her mouth, and pulled her chair out for her to sit.

"When did you have time for this?" she asked.

"I had some friends help me out." I sat opposite her, staring at her face.

"What? Do I have something on my nose? Does my breath stink?" she questioned.

I laughed at her as she grabbed a napkin to wipe her mouth. "No, I just can't help but be enamored by your beauty."

"Sounds like you're looking to get laid tonight. You don't have to work so hard."

"Well, I have plenty of tricks for the rest of the night."

"Good. But let's eat first." She lifted the top off the dish in front of her and gasped in shock at the little black box hiding underneath. Jessica picked the box up as tears pooled in her eyes.

I took it out of her hands and got down on one knee.

"Joseph..."

"Jessica, we've come a long way, and I know without a doubt I can't go on any longer without you being by my side. Would you do me the honor of being my wife?" I asked.

"Yes!" She dropped down on her knees and attacked my mouth, cheek, and forehead with kisses.

I chuckled and wrapped an arm around her waist. "Baby, I don't want a long engagement," I said.

"Me neither."

"So, what do you think of going to Vegas?" I took the ring out of the box and slid it onto her ring finger.

"You want to elope?! I guess my spontaneous ways are rubbing off on you."

"So, what do you say?"

"Let's do it tonight."

"Are you serious?"

"Well, how about next weekend? I want to enjoy making love under the moon on this boat tonight."

"I like that idea." I palmed both her ass cheeks in her dress.

"Mrs. Joseph Samuels."

"The best words I've ever heard."

* * *

One Week Later

The little white chapel was decorated with white and pink roses, and I was wearing a black tuxedo that I'd brought with me on the private jet. Jessica and I had flown out that afternoon and got a penthouse at the Venetian for our honeymoon. We came to the chapel right after our couples' spa day. She wore a white lace cocktail dress, and Tamia and Eric Benet's hit song was playing as she walked down the aisle. Once she approached the altar, I wanted to devour her heart-shaped lips, but I needed to wait until the minister finished talking.

"Do you, Joseph Michaels, take Jessica Samuels to be your lawfully wedded wife?" the minister asked.

"I do," I replied.

"Do you, Jessica Samuels, take Joseph Michaels to be your lawfully wedded husband?"

"Can I say something first?" Jessica asked.

"Of course, young lady."

"Joseph, it was you who saw the potential in me and supported me from the start. I truly believe we were meant to go through everything, so we could come out on this end. You've been the one true constant in my world, and I thank you."

The minister cleared his throat.

"Oh, and I do take you to be my husband," Jessica hastily added.

"Then by the power vested in me by the state of Nevada, I now pronounce you husband and wife. You may kiss the bride."

I lifted her hand and kissed her knuckles, then wrapped my arms around her waist, dipped her backward, and captured her lips, sealing our wedding with a kiss.

Epilogue: Jessica

One Year Later

"Congratulations!" all my friends and family shouted as I pushed the door of my new office open and allowed everyone inside.

The sign on the wall read "Samuels Graphic Designs". I smiled. I'd wanted to get a business loan and rent a place, but Joseph wouldn't hear of that and bought a standalone storefront near the car shop for me, then put everything in my name. Now, I was a proud business owner, with my own office, receptionist area, and bathroom. Once I continued to build my portfolio, I would expand. One thing I learned was to slow down and take things as they came. After living together, Joseph and I had gotten a bigger place and even purchased a home in California for when we visited Angela, Granny, and Emery.

Angela popped a bottle of champagne and poured a glass for me and the rest of the guests.

"I'm going to email you about creating a new brand design for the hair salon," Angela said.

She waved at Scarlett as she entered and approached me, holding flowers. "Congrats, boo! I'm so happy for you." Scarlett handed the flowers to me.

I took them, smelling the fresh pink roses. "Thanks. How is the life of a traveling stylist?" I rubbed her six-month baby bump. We'd always said we would wait to have kids until we hit a stride in our careers. She was now on her own as a celebrity stylist and was barely home to catch up with me. I missed my best friend but was happy to see her success in magazines and on TV shows.

"I'm swelling a lot and constantly hungry," Scarlett groaned.

Angela and I snickered at her poked-out lips. "Welcome to mommyhood. It only gets worse from here," Angela said. Scarlett gasped with her mouth wide-open.

"Angela!" I cried.

She shrugged and waved me off. "I have to be honest. Motherhood is wonderful, but sometimes Mama needs a break," Angela said and gulped the rest of her champagne.

"Where's Joseph?" Scarlett asked, ignoring Angela's comment.

"Talking to some friends over there." I pointed to Joseph, standing near my office with my brother and their friends.

"Ahhh!" Scarlett shrieked in excitement, holding my hand in hers. "When did you get married?" she questioned.

I grinned, displaying my hand out fully. "Two months ago. We flew to Vegas and got married."

She pouted. "You didn't call me. I thought we were better than that."

"Don't feel bad; you weren't the only one missing." Angela sucked her teeth in aggravation.

"Angela, I told you it was a spontaneous thing."

"I can't believe you're married," Scarlett mumbled.

"A married woman, yep."

"Wow! I'm happy for you," Scarlett said.

"Thank you."

"Scarlett, it's good to see you again." Joseph wrapped his arms around my shoulders.

"You, too. Congrats on your wedding—even though I wasn't invited." Scarlett rolled her eyes playfully, and Joseph chuckled.

"We wanted it to be private," I replied, cutting the awkwardness in the room.

"I know but maybe we can catch up before the baby is born," she said.

I reached out to give her a hug and call a truce. The both of us were moving in different directions in our lives, and we didn't need to hold onto the past and fight about things we couldn't control. I placed the flowers on the desk and watched as everyone mixed and mingled. I'd had my first appointment with another major client that Brent recommended me to—an online clothing company that was looking to launch a new design and brand style.

"What's going on in that pretty little brain of yours?" Joseph glanced over at me.

Seeing the love in his eyes warmed my heart, and I poked my lips out for a kiss. "I'm just happy."

"Mmm... tell me more." He turned and cupped both sides of my face.

"Life had a funny way of bringing us together, and I'm grateful."

"Two hearts beating as one," Joseph said.

I thought of the years we'd spent together, exploring each other's minds, bodies, and souls. I could not wait to have his kids one day or to have an anniversary party like his parents in 30 years. "Always, Mr. Michaels," I agreed.

* * *

If you want more "Mafia Romance, why not try ***"Antonio and Sabrina Book 2" Click here*** https://books2read.com/u/bpED6g

Have you read *yet **"Temptation?*** That is a stand-alone contemporary, sports, curvy girl romance. Check it out here https://books2read.com/u/mle1Vv

Are you interested in Mafia romance? Check into *Antonio & Sabrina: Struck in Love, Books 1* https://book s2read.com/u/4AxKLo

Follow a Second chance romance here "**Heart of Stone Book 3 Angela and Brent"** https://book s2read.com/u/31rx9l

Get into a One night stand romance with **Jessica and Joseph**

Heart of Stone Book 3.5 https://payhip.com/ b/HGP1

Heart of Stone Book 4 Jessica and Joseph https://books2read.com/u/4NXyPG

* * *

Check out **Aydin a grumpy boss, bodyguard romance** here https://books2read.com/u/mBwaOy .Follow my standalone opposites attract, age gap, military romance "**Exposed**" https://books2read.com/u/bQyYZe .

Are you a fan of sports romance? Then download one-night stand, billionaire romance "**Refuel**" https://books2read.com/u/boDyDA. Also, follow it up with workplace, sports romance "**Pressure**" https://books2read.com/u/3Ly1r7 .

If you love romantic comedy, fake relationships, enemies to lovers, find it here, "**Something Gained.**" Click the link https://books2read.com/u/baGLYy .

Any fan of forbidden romance, political? Check out "**Mutual Agreement**" https://books2read.com/u/mgzzWX a steamy romance. Pre-order the full novel of "**Nasir**" here click the link here.

Have you checked out "**She's All I Need**" click here https://books2read.com/u/49lkeW a sports, opposites attract romance. What about dark romance that has everything from steamy romance, opposites attract, suspense, thriller, celebrity, and more "**Joaquin Fuertes Book 1**" https://books2read.com/u/mvZlgV

Catch up with favorite characters in this holiday short romance which includes spoilers. https://books2read.com/u/bzd59G

Reading Order of series

Heart of Stone Book 1 Emery and Jackson
https://books2read.com/u/boWPAV
Heart of Stone Book 1.5
https://payhip.com/b/kWg7
Heart of Stone Book 2 Jordan and Damon
https://books2read.com/u/ba2OMx
Heart of Stone Book 3.5 Bottoms Up
https://payhip.com/b/HGP1
Heart of Stone Book 3 Angela and Brent
https://books2read.com/u/31rx9l
Heart of Stone Book 4 Jessica and Joseph
https://books2read.com/u/4NXyPG

Reading Order of Antonio and Sabrina Universe

The Early Years-A Prequel
https://books2read.com/u/49Zjnw
Ruthless Struck In Love Book 1
https://books2read.com/u/4AxKLo
Savage Struck In Love Book 2
https://books2read.com/u/bpED6g
Beast Struck In Love Book 3
https://books2read.com/u/3LpgdJ
Janice and Carlo Captivated By His Love
https://books2read.com/u/b6je6M
Brutal Struck In Love Book 4
https://books2read.com/u/4NQyE9
Stolen-Fuertes Mafia Cartel Book 1
https://books2read.com/u/mvZlgV
Saved-Fuertes Mafia Cartel Book 2
https://books2read.com/u/4DWwLd
Redemption Struck In Love Book 5
https://books2read.com/u/b5kZ8O
Betrayal- Fuertes Mafia Cartel Book 3
https://books2read.com/u/4A5LGp

Playlist:Heart of Stone Book 4

1.Tiffany Renee: Journey

2. Chicago-Hard to say I'm Sorry

3. Jazmine Sullivan-On It

4.Aretha Franklin-Shoop Shoop Song (Its In His Kiss)

5. Ariana Grande - 34+35

6.Trey Songz-We Can't be Friends

7. Usher: Here I Stand

8. Mariah Carey-We Belong Together

9. Jamie Foxx-Fall For Your Type

10. Ne-Yo: Sexy Love

About the Author

Chiquita Dennie is an author of Contemporary, Romantic Suspense, Erotic and Women's Fiction.

Chiquita lives in Los Angeles, CA. Before she started writing contemporary romance, she worked in the entertainment industry on notable TV shows such as the Dr Phil show, Tyra Banks show, American Idol, and Deal or No Deal. But her favorite job is the one she's now doing, full time writing romance.

A Best-Selling Author and Award-winning Filmmaker, her first short film "Invisible" was released in Summer 2017 and screened in multiple festivals and won for Best Short Film. She also hosts a podcast that showcases the latest in Beauty, Business and Community called "Moscato and Tea." Her debut release of Antonio and Sabrina Struck in Love has opened a new avenue of writing that she loves.

If you want to know when the next book will come out, please visit my website at http://www.chiquitadennie.com, where you can sign up to receive an email for my next release.

What's Next?

Want to know what happens next?

Follow me on this website to catch the next release.

Reviews are the lifeblood of the publishing world. They're read, appreciated, and needed.

Please consider taking the time to leave a few words on your review platform of choice.

Sign up for updates and sneak peaks at the site below.

www.chiquitadennie.com

https://www.bookbub.com/authors/chiquita-dennie? list=author_books

https://www.goodreads.com/author/show/16932446. Chiquita_Dennie?from_search=true&from_srp=true

https://304publishing.tumblr.com

www.Twitter.com/304_publishing

www.Instagram.com/304publishing

www.Facebook.com/authorchiquitadennie

304 Publishing Company

We showcase authors writing African American, Interracial, Women's Fiction, Urban Romance, Erotic, and Contemporary Romance novels. Along with Thriller, Suspense, Poetry, Beauty, and Style Books. Thank you for taking the time out to visit. Join our mailing list to stay updated with new releases and blog posts.

Thank you so much for reading and if you enjoyed the crazy ride and decide to leave a review we'd truly appreciate the support.

Catalogue of Releases

The Early Years-A Prequel Short Story
    Struck in Love 1, 2, 3,4,5
    Heart of Stone, Book 1 (Emery & Jackson)
    Heart Of Stone Book 1.5 Emery &Jackson A Valentine's Day Short
    Janice and Carlo: Captivated By His Love
    Heart of Stone, Book 2 (Jordan and Damon)
    Temptation
    Heart of Stone, Book 3 (Angela and Brent)
    Bottoms Up Heart of Stone, Book 3.5(Jessica and Joseph Short
    Cocky Catcher
    Bossy Billionaire
    Love Shorts:A Collection of Short Stories
    Stolen Fuertes Mafia Cartel Book 1
    Saved Fuertes Mafia Cartel Book 2
    Exposed (Salvation Society Novel)
    Betrayal Fuertes Mafia Cartel Book 3
    Refuel(A Driven World Novel)
    Pressure(A Driven World Novel)

Until Serena(HEA World Novel)
Exposed (Salvation Society Novel)
Heart of Stone, Book 4 (Jessica and Joseph)
She's All I Need
Something Gained(Romantic Comedy)
Thank you so much for reading, and if you enjoyed the crazy ride and decide to leave a review, we'd truly appreciate the support.

Acknowledgments

I want to dedicate this to my team that helps me behind the scenes, from my editors, test readers, graphic designers, and the list goes on. Truly appreciate each of you for keeping me on my toes.